THE GREENER GRASS & OTHER SHORT STORIES

NIKITA ABHISHEK NAYAK

THE GREENER GRASS & OTHER SHORT STORIES

NIKITA ABHISHEK NAYAK

Publishing facilitation: Brand Inspire (OPC) Pvt. Ltd
Typeset and Printing Facilitation by
Brand Inspire (OPC) Pvt. Ltd.
info@brandinspire.in

DEDICATION

My book is dedicated to my dear grandpa who isn't with us right now. He's always been my biggest inspiration to be an author without whom I wouldn't have been able to even dream about writing. I'd love to continue his legacy of writing books. I regret that I couldn't publish the book when he was here. Due to the pandemic, I kept delaying this project. I'd be honoured if my work is half as good as *Abbu's*. I'm sorry for not being as generous as him to sell my books for free. His humble attitude and generosity continue to astonish us all.

We love you *Abbu*!

Every time the wind blows over my face,
The wind chimes tinkle,
The birds chirp,
I feel his presence..
For, he's become a part of the air now.
We all know that he's in a much better place;
For he has filled his life with good karmas..
Sadly, my failed misconception about my grandparents' immortality,
Has hit me unexpectedly like a shock now..
Only living in solace for his return soon of his pure soul;
Filled with hope and faith our life is now!

-Your granddaughter

ACKNOWLEDGEMENTS

We all go through phases when we fall down and then rise back to the topmost level in life. This is when we realise that we are going to pursue our dreams no matter what. I found solace in writing and came up with stories that touch and inspire, and help survive such obstacles. Hope you all enjoy my narration and relate to some of the stories. Every story has a small takeaway that will help you connect with your life.

This wouldn't have been possible mainly without the help of my sister (Kritika Pai) who found my old manuscripts while cleaning my cupboard; so she and mom (Namita Pai) encouraged me to start writing again. They have been my reason for being an author and have always supported me in whatever I do (that story is still pending by the way, which is a psychological thriller). My dearest husband (Abhishek Nayak) was the most excited when I told him that I am going to start writing again. He has always been so supportive and encouraging. During the entire process of writing, he reviewed my manuscript every night and gave me feedback constantly. He helped me execute my dream into reality! My dad

(Kishore Pai) who's always been my guide, my second mom (Sheela Nayak) who encouraged me to write and is my great emotional support, second dad (Sunil Nayak) who reviewed my writing, and who's also my inspiration for creativity (yes, he's an actor himself), my other sister (Akshata Khot) who started circulating my work, that encouraged me. My wonderful friends who kept pushing me to write. And most importantly my dear editor, mentor and guide Rasana Atreya who is also an author of the best seller "Tell a Thousand lies". She boosted my morale and gave me a new direction. My friend Asavari and her husband Avinash, who helped me design my lovely book. Also could count upon them to guide me through the whole process of publication. I'd also like to thank my publisher Kritika Sharma from Brand Inspire who helped publish my book. ☺

TABLE OF CONTENTS

1	The Greener Grass	1
2	The 'not so obvious' Choice	9
3	The Rain of Hope	20
4	The Sacrifice	34
5	Being "Normal"	50
6	An Indian Teenager's Diary	72
7	The Uninvited Mother	84
8	The spilled cup of cappuccino!	98

THE GREENER GRASS

It was a sunny Wednesday morning. The rush to catch the local Churchgate-bound train continued at Nallasopara station. Passengers began to relax once they got onto the train. A few checked the time on their watches. The ones who got a seat looked happily out of the window. A few checked their WhatsApp messages. The rest continued to stream web series on their smartphones.

Vidya, who had managed to get a window seat, looked outside. She began to dab her face to take off the sweat with her beige cotton saree *pallu*, which her husband had gifted her when they were newly married. It had a *warli* art design at the border, something that she was very fond of. She smiled at how thoughtful her husband had been then. Her red *bindi* began to come out loose. She replaced it with another one from her purse and also redid her braid, which was loose from all the sides. She noticed that the sun had begun to hide behind the clouds. Her thoughts began to drift; her own sunny life was about to disappear because a storm was on the verge of entering it. Her perfect marriage was about to end.

Mukesh and she had met in college and fallen in love. Despite her parents' disapproval due to caste differences, they had eloped and got married secretly. After their daughter was born, her parents had finally accepted their son-in-law. Now, Vidya was a happy mother of two children, an eight-year-old daughter, and a five-year-old son. Life couldn't have been more perfect.

But everything changed one night when she spotted lipstick stains on her husband's shirt. She never wore lipstick.

His late nights at work had increased, and so had his late-night texting. Was he cheating on her?

It had been a month now. Was she procrastinating confronting him because of their children, or was it because she was afraid to face reality? That storm could destroy their lives.

The train halted at Andheri. More people crowded the train. Vidya's eyes fell on a pretty teenager dressed in a horizontal striped red and white colour t-shirt and light blue jeans, matched with a pair of brown sneakers. Her silky brown hair was tied into a high ponytail and she carried a small black backpack. Vidya remembered how wonderful life had been back in college. Mukesh and she were dating back then. Her only desire was to spend more time with him and get decent grades.

The teenager caught her staring.

Vidya looked away in embarrassment.

Ayushi, the teenager, was frustrated. Her parents were the most narrow-minded of all parents. Others her age partied like there was no tomorrow, travelled by Ubers, and did not bother about their grades. But she had to take the train, no matter how horrible the weather. And even though she was among the top ten students in her section, her parents weren't content with her grades.

If that wasn't bad enough, her deadline to be home was 7 pm. She wasn't allowed to talk to guys and wasn't allowed to wear sleeveless tops or short skirts.

She spotted a good-looking guy in the next compartment. He was the perfect example of a model who could have been selected for the Axe deodorant ads. He had the sharpest side-profile face and wore a white shirt and blue jeans with the top two buttons undone, which gave Ayushi plenty of time to imagine how amazing his body must be. He had deep black eyes and thick wavy hair. Would she ever be able to date a guy like that? Forget dating, how did it feel to even talk to a guy? How did it feel to be a guy? No restrictions for anything. Life was so much easier for guys.

Nikhil, the good-looking guy, had his struggles. He was an unappreciated hardworking employee trying hard to impress his boss. He worked hard and even stayed back late nights, but the lazy asses seemed to be getting promotions easily by licking their boss's feet. They flattered the boss and offered him gifts. Their boss was too much of a fool to understand the politics, and Nikhil was too principled a guy to do all that. He believed that his work should speak for himself.

His parents, on the other hand, were pressurizing him to get married, but he didn't own a car or a bike, and it was impossible in Mumbai to buy even a small apartment. He wished life was easier for him.

The train reached Churchgate. The crowd began to rush out of the train. It was pouring heavily. Nikhil needed to hire a taxi and reach his office, but there were too many people trying to do the same, and the taxi drivers were taking advantage of the situation by charging an unusually high fare.

Nikhil spotted a BMW pass by and cursed the woman in the backseat. She sat comfortably as her driver drove her to work. Nikhil was completely drenched by the time he managed to get a taxi. He did not reach his office on time.

It continued to pour heavily. The weather forecast looked bad, and emails from the Human Resources department began to flood his inbox, warning about the impending thunderstorm. By 3 pm, everyone began to head home. The traffic was crazy. The water-logging had already started, and it began to get dark.

Vidya and Nikhil, both of whom worked in the same office, stood close to their office building, waiting for a taxi that would take them to the train station. But it was impossible; all the offices, colleges and schools, seem to have been at the same time. They began to chat with each other, expressing their frustration. Suddenly Nikhil spotted the same BMW that he'd seen in the morning. The door opened.

There sat a gorgeous girl tailor-made for the BMW. She had heavy makeup on and her hair was set as if she'd just stepped out of a salon, thought Vidya as she looked at her own messed up hair. Her Ray-Ban shades were pulled up above her head. She was dressed formally in an olive-green velvet top and an ivory colour skirt with black stilettos.

"Do you guys need a ride to the station?" the girl asked.

"That would be wonderful," said Vidya, and got into the car. Nikhil had no option but to get into the car as well.

The girl in the car introduced herself. "Hi, I'm Meera. I have my start-up called 'Meera Life Spaces.' I live in Ruma Crown on Gokhale road. What about you guys?"

"Hi, I'm Vidya. I work at 'Senior Enterprises.' I come from Nallasopara."

"Hi, I'm Nikhil. I don't just work, but struggle at 'Senior Enterprises.'"

All three laughed at that.

"So, Nikhil, I saw you struggling in the rain this morning. I was about to ask you for a ride just as you got into a taxi," Meera said.

"These taxi *walas*, I tell you; they trouble you more during the monsoons," Vidya said.

"Yeah, we middle-class people struggle daily with these issues, but you are a lucky rich girl who owns a BMW," said Nikhil.

"Hey! Money isn't everything. Besides, it's my dad's."

"*Madam, inko station chodna hai na?*" the driver asked Meera.

"*Ji,*" replied Meera in agreement just as they saw a girl standing on the side of the road, soiled from the muddy water, asking for a ride. So Meera asked the driver to stop the car and opened the door for her.

Seeing Nikhil in the front seat, the girl, Ayushi, was excited. She thought that the car belonged to him and his driver had come to pick him due to the rains. This was her chance to talk to him. "Could you please drop me to the station?" she asked Nikhil.

"Of course, get in," said Meera.

"Oh, it's your car. Sorry."

"No worries."

Embarrassed, Ayushi reached for her phone. "Oh no! The western line is shut temporarily. A chunk of the foot over bridge has fallen on the tracks. It might take a while to fix."

"Shit, were there any deaths?" asked Vidya.

"Only injuries as of now," said Ayushi.

"I'll tell you what, guys. Come over to my place. There is going to be severe water-logging," said Meera.

"I think it's a good idea," said Ayushi, agreeing. She was excited to spend the night with the cute guy.

"No, no, my kids will be waiting for me," Vidya said.

"I'll manage on my own, but you guys go ahead. You all need to be safe," said Nikhil.

"I'm not giving anyone a choice. Driver, *ghar chalo,*" said Meera, instructing the driver to take them home.

They finally reached Meera's place in half an hour. She lived in a posh 2BHK apartment with exquisite furniture. The living room had a blue silk fabric L-shaped lounger with a glass center table, fresh lilies in a round-shaped vase. It had a huge LED glass pendant light hanging above the center table. There was a tiny bar table at the side with three high chairs and a small cabinet with Absolut

Vodka bottles, some Chivas Regal, and a Blue Label Scotch. The house smelt of lavender, with every room having a bowl of potpourri.

"What is this exactly?" asked Vidya pointing to it as they took a house tour.

The master bedroom had a king-size bed with silk bed covers and an acrylic painting of Meera behind the bed. It had a huge mirrored, sliding-door wardrobe. The bathroom had a bathtub, and the towels were nicely folded on a stand near the dry area. The guest room was smaller but equally classy, having a small bed, a wardrobe, and a side table. Everyone looked at the house in awe and finally settled on the couch in the living room.

She offered a change of clothes to the girls. And then turned to Nikhil. "I might have something for you as well. My dad keeps some of his night suits and other clothes here."

She asked her cook to bring them tea and *pakoras*. She also gave her instructions for their dinner.

"I envy your life. I hate to cook at home because of my kids' tantrums," said Vidya as she stuffed her mouth with *pakodas*.

"Your apartment is so beautiful. You have a lovely interior," said Nikhil as he tried out the furniture.

"Thanks, guys."

"Do you live by yourself?" asked Ayushi.

"Yes, my parents stay in Chandigarh."

"Wow, so lucky. My parents have so many restrictions for me. Wish I lived alone too."

As they chatted, there was a power cut. Meera got some candles from her cupboard and lit them. Then she went into the kitchen and came back with an empty bottle in her hand.

"Let's play 'spin the bottle.' The one who faces the mouth of the bottle has to answer any question that the one facing the bottom asks," she said.

Meera was the first to spin the bottle. The bottle pointed at Nikhil, and the bottom was towards Ayushi.

"So, are you single or committed?" Ayushi asked, rubbing her palms.

"Single."

"A cute guy like you, and single!" Ayushi exclaimed.

"You need money to impress girls. I'm not even settled yet."

"Money isn't everything, Nikhil. Ayushi has been trying to take a shot at you, but all you do is sulk," said Meera.

"I'm sorry, you guys don't understand. We men need to settle well before we start dating. We need to fulfil our woman's needs."

"I agree Nikhil, but money is not everything," said Meera as Ayushi spun the bottle.

Now it was Meera's turn to ask Vidya a question.

"Since you've had a love marriage, please tell us the story of how you met."

Vidya narrated her story, and everyone began to clap after she finished. Vidya began to look pale.

"Are you alright? Did we make you uncomfortable?" Meera asked.

"No, no, not at all."

Now the bottle pointed to Meera, and it was Nikhil's turn to ask a question.

"So Meera, you have a perfect luxurious life. Do you still feel like you are missing out something in your life?"

"Of course, I do. I wish I had my own family."

"What do you mean?" asked Nikhil.

"I have a weak heart due to which my health isn't great. So, I have decided not to ever get married. I don't want to ruin someone else's life, and I don't want my parents taking care of me their whole life either. Therefore, I choose to live alone. It's very complicated guys. A husband and two children are what I miss."

"I'm so sorry to hear that, Meera." Vidya took Meera's hand in hers.

"I'm sorry for asking you that question," said Nikhil, and Ayushi got up and offered Meera a hug.

"You are indeed lucky," said Meera, turning to Vidya.

"No, I'm not! I think my husband's cheating on me." Vidya broke down.

"I'm so sorry. I didn't know," said Meera apologetically.

Vidya rested her head on Meera's shoulder and began to sob.

It was at that moment that everyone realised how they had their battles to fight, and that the grass always looks greener on the other side.

Vidya would soon confront her husband but give him a second chance because she didn't want to be alone.

Meera realised that picture-perfect families weren't always perfect.

Ayushi realised that her life was so much better. She promised herself that she wouldn't grumble about her parents.

As for Nikhil, he was just dumbfounded. He finally realised that money wasn't the solution to everything. From now on, he would live his life to the fullest. Probably hang out more often with his friends. It was also at that point, that he noticed Ayushi and realised how pretty she was. She didn't give up flirting with him, even though she knew he wasn't rich. He would probably ask her on a date when the two were alone. He had his whole life ahead of him to make money, but his youth would be there for a short while only.

THE 'NOT SO OBVIOUS' CHOICE

"It's such a beautiful clear day today," thought Revati, as she looked up at the sky. She was sitting in the back of her office cab, on her way to work. She was modestly dressed in an orange cotton kurti with a flower print on it, matched with a pair of light green leggings. She had pinned up her crown of hair and the rest was left loose. It was a Monday morning and everyone was busy catching up on the latest episode of "Game of Thrones" season finale. The cab was moving at a snail's pace towards the Silk Board junction.

"I hate the traffic in Bangalore," she grumbled.

Revati was a twenty-four-year-old lean girl who had caramel-coloured cheeks that flushed every time she was excited or nervous. She never wore makeup except for her favourite strawberry lip balm and the thin line of kajal under her eyes.

She lived in Bangalore in BTM layout as a paying guest. Her family lived in Marathahalli but due to the long-distance travel, she'd moved out. She had been recruited by Infosys through a campus interview. After rigorous training in Mysore, she was posted in Bangalore. Everyone in her family was proud of her, but she was not content with her job. She wanted to achieve something more. "Everyone gets a job after college, and just because I did well academically doesn't mean I'm smart. I need to win over my boss's respect too. I'm a nobody in this huge company," she thought. It was two years now, and her family wanted her to start looking at guys, so she was forced to register on *shaadi* and all the matrimonial websites that ever existed.

Revati had told her parents that she would happily marry, but she wanted to achieve something in life first. Her parents ignored her and continued the search for suitable grooms. She was a cheerful girl, but the pressure to shine was making her sullen. Her family and friends were unhappy at the sudden change in her attitude towards life. Everyone tried their best to make her understand that she should not run behind success all the time and it would come to her eventually due to her hard work, but it was all in vain.

Finally, the cab reached the campus and everyone headed towards the office building to swipe their cards and then went to the cafeteria for breakfast. Revati sat alone for her meals. She isolated herself from everyone because she thought that people distracted her from her focus on work. She read Forbes magazine during breakfast. Women leaders around the world inspired her and helped her focus on her own goals. After breakfast, she started working on the tasks her team lead had assigned her.

"Please submit a little late today. Your team says that you are a threat to all," said John, the team lead, laughing.

"I don't care if they are lazy and slow," Revati snapped.

"Just kidding. Chill."

Revati began her task at once and was completely engrossed when, around 11 o'clock, her *amma* called her up.

"Hi, Revati. No call from you today."

"*Amma*, I'm busy with work. Can we talk in the evening?"

"Sure, just listen to me once. Shetty Uncle was saying that he has a guy for you in mind. He is well settled, and from a good family."

"Who's not, *Amma!*"

"Just check out his profile on *shaadi*. I will also share his LinkedIn profile because I know that the work profile interests you a lot more." Her *amma* laughed.

"I will, *Amma*. Now, can I get back to work, please?"

"Okay, and please don't skip lunch, okay? You do that often, I know."

"*Amma*, please, *yaar*. I'm busy. Bye."

After work that evening, Revati checked out the guy's LinkedIn profile just to get her *amma* off her back. She was surprisingly impressed with it. His name was Shubham Shastri. He had more recommendations from his bosses and colleagues than her. He was a star performer in his team and had an MS degree from the U.S. He had also been a topper in his class since his school days. His *shaadi* profile mentioned that he was looking for an independent working woman, and would have no restrictions on her career or her clothing. She immediately called her *amma*.

"*Amma*, I am okay meeting the guy, but only to get you off my back."

"*Haha. Nange munche inda ne gottitu.* You loved his LinkedIn profile, didn't you?"

"*Amma*, please."

The horoscopes were matched and the families decided that the couple should meet each other before the families met.

They decided to meet at a restaurant in Meenakshi mall one evening.

Shubham was a shy guy by nature. He did well academically but was average on looks, his focus was more on the little things that gave him happiness. He always dressed in plain t-shirts and dull coloured shirts. He never paid attention to his looks or dressing, just like Revati. He always put family and friends over money or his work. He respected women and wanted his wife to have her career. He felt that the household chores should be equally distributed amongst the couple. He had seen how his *amma* had given up her job to take care of the kids, and how she ran around the house doing errands for everyone while his *appa* only ordered her around. His *appa* refused to even pick up his plate after meals. Shubham always wanted to put an end to this patriarchal mind-set.

The minute he saw Revati in the photos that her mother sent, he had fallen in love with her. It wasn't just her looks. Something about her told him that she would be his future wife; the mother of his children; the person to keep his family together, the one who would put family over everything else just like he did. The day they met, he was confident about his perceptions of her. Revati seemed very confident and spoke about herself in detail. She did not hesitate to ask him anything about his career, but he noticed that she did not ask him a single question about his personal life.

A few days after their coffee date, they met for dinner at UB City. It was a Friday night. Shubham finally opened his heart and told her that he was in love with her.

Revati smiled. She said that she was also very happy to marry him, but she had a condition. She would only get married once she'd fulfilled her dreams of achieving a breakthrough in her career.

"Take all the time in the world. I am in no hurry. I always respect women who chase their dreams," Shubham said.

"Thank you for understanding me."

"Isn't there anything you want to ask me about my personal life? I asked you so many questions."

"*Nah, ma* has told me everything I need to know about you and your family." She smiled.

The families met, and the marriage was official. Shubham's parents knew that Revati didn't want to set a date immediately, so it was agreed that they would be ready whenever Revati was.

At first, the courtship period was fun for Shubham. They met frequently on weekends and also had a few fun trips with friends, but Revati changed the subject every time he spoke about a date for their wedding. It had been months now and his parents kept asking if they had picked a date. Shubham was ready to wait, but he needed to know about her plans. She got upset every time the topic came up.

One fine day, Revati called him up. She sounded excited. This had been the first time she'd been so happy since he'd met her.

"I'm getting the 'Employee of the Year' award," she said thrilled.

"Wow."

"Yeah, it's a new tradition that started a couple of years ago and I'm the first woman to receive this award."

"Great, I'm happy for you Revati, you've always wanted to achieve something. Hope this satisfies your expectations."

"Oh yeah. I've never been so happy."

"Not even when you met me?"

"C'mon now. Don't be so emotional. You know me. Career always comes first."

The conversation ended up in an argument where Revati accused him of being jealous and upsetting her mood on such an important day. Shubham was forced to apologise, though he didn't think he was guilty of anything. He was starting to worry now. It wasn't just about picking a date for the wedding. He wondered if Revati was only getting married because of societal pressure. Were his instincts about her wrong? But she was happy about her award right now, so he decided not to bother her for a couple of days. Except for a few greetings during the day, there wasn't much conversation between the two.

One day Revati unexpectedly dropped by his apartment. It was a lazy Saturday afternoon and his flatmates were still sleeping. Shubham had just woken up and was having tea.

"Hi, you woke up so late?" She smiled as he opened the door for her.

"Yeah, c'mon in."

"You want to go for lunch?"

Shubham quickly showered, and they left for the Rajdhani restaurant. He was very happy that she wanted to spend time with him.

"So how have you been doing? I've missed you," said Shubham.

"I'm good. Yeah, me too. Hey, listen, *na*. Please tell me how my speech for the award ceremony is. I've been rehearsing it so much and now I want somebody's opinion on it."

"Is that why you wanted to meet me?"

"Of course not, don't be silly. Also, we need to pick a dress for me for the occasion."

"Okay Revati, we will do everything you want. But you promised me that after you achieved something in your career, you'd pick a wedding date."

"Oh yes. I will talk to *amma* tonight and ask her to speak to our *pandit ji* and he'll pick a date in the next three months. Is that cool with you?"

"Yes, it is. But are you excited about getting married? I hope you're not just doing it for me and your parents. You know I always respect a woman's career as she is suppressed by society but I don't want my wife to be unhappy after marriage."

"No, no, I'm happy to get married Shubham. Why are you asking me that? Is it because of our fight the other day? I'm really sorry about the stuff I said." She touched his hand.

That night Revati couldn't sleep. She was very excited about her award ceremony. In her mind, she wore the dress she'd picked, and kept rehearsing her speech over and over. She would first thank her parents and then her fiancé for all the support she had got from them. And most importantly, her paternal grandmother who she'd been the closest to.

Her *ajji* was the one who had always been by Revati's side throughout her childhood. Revati shared everything with her. Whenever she had any concerns in school with her friends or teachers, she discussed them with the older lady. Her *amma* was a little envious of their relationship, but Revati was more comfortable with her *ajji* than anyone else in the world. She remembered how her *ajji* had supported her when she applied for her first job, even as her parents were forcing her to get married first. Finally, after texting Shubham that her speech was ready and sending him a picture of herself in the new dress, she dozed off.

Shubham couldn't sleep that night. Revati didn't seem interested in the wedding, treating it like it was something distasteful that had to be done. She was happier about her award and her speech than anything else. He expressed his concern to his *amma*, with whom he rarely shared his anxiety with.

"She seems more interested in the award than getting married to me, *Amma*. I don't think she's even interested in getting married. For her, career and fame seem everything."

"I'm sure that's not the case, dear. In our country, women are quite suppressed so she's just happy about proving to the world that women are much more than just housewives."

"But the obsession is too much, *Amma*. I support her dreams, but family should always come first to anyone whether man or woman."

"We've met her, dear. She seems sensible. I'm sure it's just a phase. Give her some time. I'm sure once the award ceremony is over, she'll get excited about the wedding as well. It's a big day for every woman. Also, her *amma* had called saying that we have good dates like 12th and 20th November, 25th and 29th December. We can have the engagement on the previous day. They prefer the 29ᵗʰ date as it's a Sunday. What do you say?"

"What does Revati want?"

"She also prefers a Sunday so that her friends and colleagues can attend the wedding."

"I will have a word with Revati once she finishes with her award ceremony before I finalise anything."

"Sure, you can, but I'm sure there's nothing to be worried about. Goodnight."

"Goodnight, *Amma*."

It was the evening before the award ceremony. Revati was anxiously pacing up and down in her apartment. Her best friend's wedding was on the same day as her award ceremony. She recollected how she'd told her that she had something more important to do. Her friend sounded upset over the phone and asked her to at least attend her *sangeet* and *mehendi* ceremonies, but Revati had refused, saying that she had some preparations to do. Her friend hadn't said much but Shubham, who was with her at the time, got very upset and said that she didn't have to be so rude. He was texting her now, reminding her of her friend's *sangeet*. She didn't care. Everybody got married, it wasn't a big deal. But achieving something on your own was the real deal, especially for her, since people had always underestimated her. She wanted to prove to everyone that they were all wrong. She'd post the video recording of her speech on her Facebook page. There was no way she'd miss something like this for some stupid wedding, not even her own. Her *pandit ji* had even picked an engagement date for tomorrow but she'd asked *amma* not to mention it to anybody and keep the engagement on the day before the wedding. If Shubham got to know about this, there would be unnecessary drama.

Finally, the big day arrived but Revati was upset; she hadn't slept a wink the previous night. She couldn't afford to be sick on her big day, so she gulped a Crocin. The thought of missing the ceremony made her nauseous. She'd invited her parents and Shubham for the ceremony as she was allowed to bring guests. The event would start at 6 pm and her award would be given around 7 pm, so she'd asked them to reach an hour early. She'd told her *appa* and Shubham to record her speech separately on their phones. She needed backup in case one of the phones froze or in case the battery died.

At 5 pm she peeped from backstage and saw Shubham sitting quietly. There was no emotion on his face. He seemed very off since the whole award thing had come up. She'd have a word with him about this. He wasn't one of the jealous male chauvinistic guys, but something was bothering him. Was it her behaviour?

She knew she'd been giving this award way more importance than anything else. She didn't want to lose him. She'd talk to him first thing tomorrow and clear everything up. After half an hour, she peeped again. Her parents were nowhere in sight. Were they caught up in traffic? They were supposed to come with Shubham. She had to call them up and make sure they reached on time.

Revati's parents had told Shubham to go ahead, saying that they would come in a little later. Her *appa* seemed a little off on the phone. Shubham repeatedly asked him what the matter was to which he replied that everything was alright. It was 7 pm now and the award distribution had started.

Then the strangest thing happened. Shubham heard the announcement for "Employee of the Year," but Revati did not appear on stage.

Shubham was taken aback. Where could she have gone? She'd waited for this moment and obsessed endlessly over it for the past few weeks. She had even sent a picture of herself from backstage saying that she was excited about the evening. After two minutes, a request was made for Revati's fiancé Shubham to collect the award on her behalf.

He collected the award for her but did not say anything on stage as he was so shocked. He stared at the award in his hand. It was a curved golden bust of a confident woman staring at him. He went outside and dialled Revati's number. There was no response. So he called her *appa*.

"Hi uncle, where is Revati? She didn't come to receive the award."

"I'm sorry, Shubham, we didn't have time to inform you. My *amma* had a minor stroke and had to be admitted. We tried to hide it from Revati but she kept asking, so we told her to come to the hospital after the ceremony because her *ajji* was doing okay and was stable, but she just left everything and rushed to the hospital. Her *ajji* means the world to her…"

Shubham was dumbstruck. He had been judging this girl all the while for giving her career way too much importance and all of a sudden, she'd made the most unexpected quick decision on the most important day of her life. Wasn't this the kind of girl he'd always wanted to marry? The kind who tossed aside everything for her family? He smiled to himself as he'd made the perfect choice. His *amma* had been right after all. Women are so suppressed that they always need to prove themselves. It didn't mean that they didn't want to have their own family. They didn't always have to choose. His doubts had been all in vain.

"Shubham? Are you there?"

"Yes, I'm coming to the hospital, please message me the address."

Shubham hugged Revati the minute he saw her at the hospital. She looked beautiful in the blue gown she'd carefully chosen. He remembered how she'd told him that she'd look more confident in the colour. Her face reminded him of the first time he had seen her in the pictures. The girl who'd be his future wife, the mother of his children; the person to keep his family together, the one who put family over everything else.

"I'm so sorry, Shubham; I left without even informing you. I was in a hurry. I hope you're not mad at me for leaving you. I wasn't sure what the right thing to do was. I love my *ajji* so much." She said wiping her tears. Her kajal smudged over her face.

"Don't worry, I'm not mad. We both made the best choice today. Here is your much-deserved award," he said, wiping her tears as she looked at him confused.

THE RAIN OF HOPE

As Yashwant stood with a glass of scotch at his friend's yearly rooftop party, he looked at the sky above. It thundered ferociously, tearing apart the Delhi skyline. Two years ago he had looked up at the same sky and begged the rain gods for mercy. He had wished for a little more sunshine in his life, even as things were falling apart.

Yashwant lived in New Delhi with his family that consisted of his mother, wife, son, and daughter-in-law. Their house was a 3BHK apartment that they had moved into after his son's marriage. The apartment had a big living room and a small dining room. The kitchen was opposite the dining room, beside it was the master bedroom, and the other two bedrooms faced each other. They had moved all the old wooden furniture to their new house, which gave it a very simple appearance.

Yashwant was a humble man who never dyed his grey hair and beard. His favourite pastime was to listen to Mohammed Rafi's songs on his Caravan which his daughter-in-law, Kavya, had gifted him when his CD player stopped working. He was smart-looking with dark brown eyes, tall and broad shoulders. His son, Akash was a younger and fitter version of him, except for the blue eyes that he'd inherited from his grandmother. Yashwant's mother Lalita, was quite modern compared to her daughter-in-law Sarita, who wore plain cotton sarees and tied her hair in a simple bun. Sarita wore gold bangles and her only social outings were family functions and *Mata ki Chowkis*. She loved cooking; her *aloo ke parathe, sarson ka saag, and rajma chawal* topped her menu. Whereas Lalita dyed her hair, and never missed her facial appointments. She liked to dress in jeans and kurtas or salwaar suits. She was a principal in a private school where she continued working even after retirement. She had her kitty parties and did social work at the club. She was never at home and hated cooking. She never stepped foot in the kitchen after Yashwant's marriage.

Akash, a qualified CA, was married two years ago and worked at a start-up. Kavya was also a CA and worked in Ernst and Young. She was very good-looking with long straight hair and a fair complexion. She had big round black eyes, a perfectly shaped nose, and full lips. She had a great figure and carried any outfit confidently. They both had met in college, dated for several years, and got married after they had settled down at their respective jobs. Kavya had recently announced her pregnancy eleven weeks ago, and everyone at home was very excited.

It all started when Lalita had a fall in the bathroom.

"*Meri zindagi khatam ho gayi*; I cannot be at home. I need to keep working till I die. This is a slow, painful death." She cried bitterly in Yashwant's arms.

"But *Ma*, your health is more important. You need to consider retirement."

"I cannot just sit at home and do nothing."

"You can help Sarita with the household chores."

"I finish my work early morning and leave; I don't need a whole day to do that."

"Your daughter-in-law has always been at home."

"She's very slow with her work."

"*Ma*, you don't have to criticise me for everything." Sarita appeared in the room with some medicines.

"Sorry, I'm just frustrated."

"Please take these medicines and rest. We will figure something out."

That night, Yashwant spoke to Sarita about his concerns.

"*Ma* is not used to being at home; she's going to be lashing out at you more often. I'm concerned about the situation."

"You worry over little things, Yashwant; I will deal with her and find something for her."

There was a scream from Akash's room. They knocked on his door frantically.

"Akash, is everything alright?"

They heard sobs as Akash opened the door for them.

"We need to take Kavya to the hospital. She's getting unbearable cramps."

"I'll come with you," said Sarita.

The three of them drove to the hospital, and Kavya was rushed inside. After thirty minutes of anxious waiting, the doctor reappeared. She signalled them to come to her cabin.

"I'm sorry, Akash. I have unfortunate news. We lost the baby."

"Are... are you sure?" Akash stammered in shock.

"Yes, I'm very sorry."

"Is Kavya okay?"

"Yes, she's resting. You can take her home tonight."

Sarita placed her hand on Akash's shoulders. It was just recently that they had celebrated the good news. Yashwant had bought a cute baby poster for their room even though Kavya warned them that it was too soon to celebrate and she had to complete at least twelve weeks. Little did they know that things would end like this.

"Does she need to be operated upon?" asked Akash.

"No. A D&C won't not be necessary."

"Is there a reason for this to have happened?" Sarita asked the doctor.

"Not that I could find any. Usually, the first twelve weeks are critical. But the good news is that they can try again after a short break. We will run some tests. Depending on the results, we can give her blood thinners and progesterone shots if required. We shall do thorough monitoring the next time. Don't worry, Aunty. It's all going to be okay," she consoled them.

The three of them drove home gloomily. Yashwant was waiting anxiously at the door. Sarita told him about it as Kavya sat on the couch weeping.

"I'm sorry, *Beta*," said Sarita, holding her hand.

"Never thought something like this would ever happen to us," said Yashwant.

"We can try again, the doctor seems very sure," Akash tried to console her.

"A loss is always a loss," said Kavya wiping her tears.

The next day at breakfast, Kavya appeared dressed in formals, ready to go to work.

"*Beta*, are you sure you want to go to work? You can rest for a couple of days," Sarita said.

"No, I'm fine," she replied brusquely.

Akash signalled Sarita not to say anymore.

"I'll drop you today, don't take the metro," said Akash.

"I don't need special treatment, Akash. As I said, I'm totally fine."

The next couple of days were tough for everyone. Kavya refused to speak to anyone and snapped every time anyone asked her anything. Yashwant and Sarita made sure Kavya got all the space she needed to grieve.

One night after dinner, when Sarita and Yashwant were in their room preparing for bed, there was a knock on the door. It was

Kavya. She looked very pale, and the dark blue circles below her eyes were very visible. She wore no makeup and had left her hair loose.

"I saw a dream last night. A beautiful boy, with blue eyes like Akash's, appeared in my arms. He started crying, and I couldn't find a way of calming him. He said that he didn't want to leave me, and was very scared. I assured him that I would protect him but he said there was nothing I could do when the time came." She began to weep profusely.

Sarita held her tightly and began to cry as well.

"We are all puppets in front of God. There's nothing we can do, Kavya. But the good news is that you can conceive again very soon," Yashwant said, as he tried to console her.

"Yes, *Papa*, but I can never have my baby back."

From that day on, the atmosphere at home was very depressing. Lalita refused to speak to anyone and sulked in her room all day as she was stuck home. Kavya, who had been the bubbliest person at home, refused to even smile. She spoke very little. The worse to come was when Akash was fired from his job only a month after the miscarriage. The start-up was shutting down and they couldn't afford to pay their employees anymore. The rains had begun now, and the city was getting very dark.

"The darkness has matched our home," Yashwant said.

"Why don't we all take a vacation?" suggested Sarita.

"I'm not sure if anyone would agree."

That night during dinner, Sarita suggested at the table.

"*Papa* and I were thinking that we should all take a vacation. You guys pick a place."

"I'm out. I cannot take a leave, especially in this situation," said Kavya.

"What do you mean by this situation?" Akash asked. "You think I'm not trying enough to get a new job, Kavya?"

"I didn't say that Akash, but my job is critical for us, especially when you are sitting at home."

"I'm struggling hard. I've got a couple of interviews lined up next week. It's not easy to get a job as a CA."

"I'm a CA too. It's not that difficult either. I got a job interview for you today. You missed it only because your lazy ass woke up late."

"Just shut up, Kavya. It's not easy being at home. Especially when your *papa* and wife go off to work, and you're running errands for *mummy*."

"Yeah, I hate it too. Sarita gives me most of the cooking since our cook, Meena is absent from work," said Lalita.

"Shelling garlic and peas aren't cooking, *Ma*. Besides, I wanted to keep you both occupied. I'm sorry, I shall manage everything myself till Meena comes back," Sarita said.

"Sorry *Mummy*, I will also help you," said Kavya.

"Don't worry, *Beta*. You have to go to work."

"Wow, *Mummy*. Thanks again for reminding me that I'm idle," said Akash.

"Stop it, everyone," shouted Yashwant finally. He'd been quiet all this time. "I know everyone is having a hard time but, please, let's not hurl allegations at each other. Sarita was only suggesting the vacation to make you all feel better. She's always wanted everyone to be happy. If you don't want the vacation, we will not go. But please stop the bickering."

Everyone ate quietly and went to bed. They would usually all watch TV after dinner, but it was only Sarita and Yashwant that night.

Yashwant expected things to get better the next day, but it did not. Lalita continued her sarcasm toward Sarita, but Sarita didn't say a single word. The fights between Kavya and Akash had gone from bad to worse. They could hear the shouting from their room, and the doors being slammed.

One night, at midnight, Kavya came out from her room and sat on the couch beside Yashwant. He'd fallen asleep in the living room with the newspaper in his hand.

"*Papa.*" She shook him. "Please go inside and sleep."

"What are you doing here at this time, *Beta?*"

"I couldn't sleep. Akash and I have been fighting a lot lately."

"Yes, we all have noticed. You both are having a hard time, but this isn't the way of dealing with the situation."

"But he just sits around and does nothing. And then his empty mind becomes a devil's workshop. He keeps saying I come home late on purpose, and don't spend enough time with him. You know how critical my job is when he's not working. It's been months now, *Papa.*"

"I will talk to him tomorrow. Meanwhile, why don't you go visit your parents for a couple of days? You hardly meet them."

"I've too much work. Are you trying to get rid of me because of the fights?"

"No, Kavya. I want you to have a change of atmosphere, especially after the incident. Your *mummy* called Sarita the other day. She was concerned about you. You barely talk to anyone, *Beta.*"

"I haven't told her about Akash losing his job yet. I'm scared she'll be worried."

"Why, Kavya? She's your *mummy.* It's very hard for us parents to see our kids suffer alone."

"*Hmm.* I'll go tomorrow and stay over for a couple of days. I can travel to work from there. I know I've not met them for a long time. I'm just avoiding the visits because I don't want them to see me like this."

"Good, now please go to bed."

The next day there was an aroma of *gobi parathas* in the house.

"Wow, who's making them?" Yashwant went to the kitchen.

"I'm making them. I haven't cooked for a while," said Kavya.

Akash seemed very happy.

"You woke early to make my favourite breakfast?" he asked cheerfully.

"Yes, you have an important interview. I want you to go with a tummy full," said Kavya smiling.

"*Bahut he ache bane hai beta*," said Sarita, licking her fingers.

"By the way, I'm thinking of visiting *mummy papa* for a couple of days," said Kavya.

"Sure Kavya, you don't need my permission," said Akash.

After breakfast, Yashwant spoke to Akash.

"Akash, I suggested to Kavya that she should visit her parents."

"Okay."

"Kavya's still not over the miscarriage. It's very hard for a woman to forget something like this, plus all the work pressure is getting to her. You need to understand her sometimes."

"I've lost the child too, *Papa*. I hate being jobless as well, but it's not easy to find a job. It makes me frustrated."

"You knew the risks when you joined a start-up. You told me millennials like taking risks, unlike us. See how stable my job is?"

"No offense, *Papa*, but you are doing a clerical job. You hardly make anything."

"Yes, I am aware. But it's the stability that I get."

"I will get a job soon too, don't worry. Wish me luck for today."

"Good luck, Akash."

The atmosphere had started to get a little normal. Akash kept himself busy with some sport or activity. He spent his morning job surfing. One night after dinner, when they were all watching TV and eating *gulab jamun*, they heard the doorbell.

Sarita went to open the door. She was shocked to see her daughter, Ahana.

She stood there totally drenched in the rains with her eyeliner dripping down her eyes. She was dressed in denim shorts, a red tank top, and flip-flops. She had a leather handbag on her right shoulder while she held a trolley bag in her left hand.

She had a fair complexion, like Sarita and had delicate features and brown wavy hair that fell over her shoulders. The minute she saw her *mummy*, she hugged her and started weeping.

"What happened? Where's Rohit?"

"He's home."

"Did you drive alone so late in the night? What happened? Will you say something?"

"I'm done with Rohit. I'm done with the marriage." Ahana wept uncontrollably as she dragged her bag in.

Yashwant went toward her nervously, and everyone else just stared in shock.

"Please go and change. You are drenched. We'll talk about it calmly."

After Ahana had changed, she sat cross-legged on the floor and narrated how Rohit had changed after marriage. She said he ignored her for his friends, and the late nights at work were also out of control. She felt neglected and got bored at home since she wasn't working.

"You're crazy. Always wanting attention. The poor guy is providing for you. You do nothing all day and yet crib," Akash shouted.

"What do you do these days, anyway? Kavya provides for you, isn't it, Akash?" Ahana lashed out.

"Calm down, kids. Aahu, these are very small things that can be worked out. It's only been a year. You both need time to get to know each other. Who leaves home late at night like this? Hope he at least knows you're here," Sarita said.

"Who do you think sent me here?"

"I'm sure Rohit would never do that. *Beta*, please rest now. If you want, you can stay for a couple of days," said Yashwant.

"Couple of days? Is this the kind of support my family gives me? If I'm such a burden, I'll find my place."

"That's not what *papa* meant, *Beta*. You cannot give up on marriage so easily." Sarita got up to follow her daughter as she ran to her room.

"Still so immature," Akash murmured.

"Sarita, she's tired. Leave her alone for tonight," said Yashwant.

The next couple of weeks were messy again. The bickering between the siblings had gone out of control. Sarita tried her best to keep them apart. Sarita and Yashwant were very concerned about their children. Ahana kept insisting on a divorce. Then, one afternoon, Yashwant got a call from Akash in the afternoon.

"*Papa, mummy* fainted today. I've called the doctor. Please come home as soon as possible."

Yashwant rushed home. The worst scenarios kept occurring to him, but he tried to calm himself down. He went to their room. Sarita was resting.

"Are you okay? What happened?"

"I'm fine. Dr Mukherjee examined me. He said my B.P. dropped."

"You worry too much, Sarita."

"I'm worried about our kids. Ahana wants a divorce. She's ruining her life, and Akash isn't getting a job. Plus the miscarriage. It's too much to process. This year has been the worst for us."

"Yeah, that's true, but there's nothing much we can do about it. Only pray to God that it gets only better from here. It cannot get worse than this."

"Every time I think like that, something else happens. I'm so fed up with everything. Everyone is at each other's throats all the time."

"I've tried talking to Rohit, but he says he's not ready to talk yet. He needs some air, is what he says."

"Do you think he wants a divorce as well? Do his parents know about it?" asked Sarita.

"I don't know anything. Aahu isn't listening to anybody. I tried talking to her so many times. I hope both of them come halfway or it's going to be very difficult."

"Yeah."

"Meanwhile, you please rest. We will do everything we can from our side, but the rest is up to God. When things aren't in our hands, we can only hope and pray for things to get better," Yashwant said.

A few days later, Kavya was home. Akash picked her up and told her about Ahana on the way, so she did not show any astonishment and behaved normally with her.

Kavya tried to drop subtle hints by giving Ahana the example of her friends, and how they'd dealt with their marriages.

"Kavya, I know you mean well, but I don't feel like being married. I was too young and took a hasty decision. We'd just met in college and I was too desperate to get married. I didn't even want a career. Now I feel that I should have spent more time in accomplishing something."

"It's never too late, Aaha. We can still find something for you. Don't you love makeup? The other day you did my makeup and I remember telling you that it was the work of a professional. You can sign up for these courses and have your salon. It's so 'in' these days to do stuff like bridal makeup, etc."

"Not a bad idea, Kavu."

"That way you will be engaged and your issues also will be resolved."

"*Mein kabhi wapas nahi jaaungi.*"

The doorbell rang. Kavya went to answer the door.

"Well, well. Look who's here, Aaha."

"Hi Ahana," said Rohit from the door.

"Come in, Jiju."

One look at him and Ahana ran off to her room.

Rohit was a well-built guy with lean shoulders. He had a dusky complexion and could easily pass off for a hunk. He had the darkest eyes with thick eyelashes. He was dressed in a fancy printed-checks blue shirt and black jeans. His hair was neatly combed and pulled back with hair gel. He smelled of heavy cologne.

"Still angry?" Rohit asked Kavya.

"Yes. What did you do?"

"I didn't do anything. She keeps threatening about leaving me and going to her parents' place. So, one day I said go. And here we are." He smiled.

"Very bad, Jiju. This isn't the way to handle a woman."

"Kavya, you're not the right person to tell a man how to handle his woman." Akash stepped into the living room.

"Oh ya! You are the person who knows everything," snapped Kavya.

Just then Sarita and Yashwant entered the living room.

"Look who's here, Ahana," shouted Sarita.

"She knows. That's why she ran off," said Rohit.

"Can we please talk about this?" said Yashwant to Rohit.

"Yes, *Papa*. Ahana is at home all day. She doesn't want to work nor do the household chores. She gets bored all day and so she expects me to come home early and spend more time with her. But it's not possible, I've got a job. I cannot come early every day. She thinks that we're still in college and wants to take trips any time she wants to. I tried to do everything to please her, but she needs to understand that we're adults now. Life isn't like how it was when we were dating."

"You are right, Rohit," Yashwant said. "I do understand what you're trying to say, but Ahana is just twenty-two. I'd always asked her to settle down in a job before she got married, but she didn't listen to me, and now she's bored. She expects you to be the same college boyfriend that you were."

"Don't mind me interfering but, Jiju, love shouldn't fade after marriage. You always missed classes for her. Now you need to try and show her you still feel the same way," Kavya said.

"But he's got work and responsibilities, Kavya. He can't just step out from work anytime he wants. He's the breadwinner for them both. Now I realise how much I've troubled you for the past couple of months. I'm sorry."

"No Akash, I was very frustrated too. All you asked me to do is spend time with you. I didn't realise how bored you got at home."

Yashwant and Sarita smiled at each other. Just then Ahana came out.

"I heard your conversation. I'm sorry, Rohit. I shouldn't have left home and come here."

"It's my fault. I shouldn't have let you go."

"What made you take so long to come and get me?"

"Ego! I'm sorry. I've taken a couple of days off. I'm taking you on a short vacation."

"Awesome. I'm also planning to start my salon. Kavya gave me this idea. I want to be occupied. I want a career now."

"Sure. Pack your bags. Let's go."

That night in bed, Yashwant spoke to Sarita.

"See, I told you God would take care of everything."

"Yes, I'm so happy all four of them have resolved their issues on their own."

The next morning, Kavya gave them more good news. She was expecting again.

She took great care of herself through the months of her pregnancy. Akash also got a job almost immediately. Kavya gave birth to a boy. Everyone at home was very happy. When she had to get back to work after her maternity leave was over, Lalita volunteered to take care of the baby. She was happy to be occupied by her great-grandson and wasn't feeling trapped at home anymore.

It started pouring, and Yashwant's glass of scotch began to fill with rainwater. He smiled to himself. The rains had given back everything that they had taken away two years ago. Life is always a full circle. Whatever you lose, you get back. Dark tunnels that seem endless always end at some point. Every night is followed by day. Every room has a door somewhere. Never lose hope; life means possibilities.

Yashwant's friend came out looking for him. "You are drenched. Dinner is served. Do you want to change before you eat?"

"I think I should head back home. It's getting late. My grandson doesn't sleep if I'm not home," said Yashwant.

"You're a lucky man." His friend smiled.

THE SACRIFICE

As the sun began to set, Harshika's heart started beating faster. She had a test tomorrow at school for which she had not studied. She needed to act fast to skip it.

"*Aaoo*," she cried as she walked to the kitchen.

"What happened, Harsha?" Sudha, asked.

"*Mamma*, my stomach is hurting suddenly," Harsha said, holding her tummy.

"What did you eat? Shall I give you medicine?"

"No. I'm going to lie down for a bit."

"Okay."

At dinner time, Sudha went to Harshika's room with a bowl of curd rice. "Have this, you will feel better."

"Thank you, *Mamma*." Harsha opened her eyes.

She began to eat slowly, holding her stomach with one hand. "*Ooh, ooh!*"

"What happened, *Beta*?"

"I have a test tomorrow and I can't study now; my tummy is still hurting."

"Don't worry; I'll give you some medicine, it will make you feel better and you can study tonight."

"But it's too late now. The medicine will take at least an hour to work. It's already 9 pm, *Mamma*."

"Okay, you rest, good night."

Harsha smiled to herself. It was too easy to fool *mamma*.

At the dinner table, Sudha spoke to Naren about Harshika. "Harsha wanted to escape some test in school so she pretended to be sick."

"Last month her teacher complained to us about her poor grades, remember? That's why she wants to skip the test. This isn't her first time," said Naren.

"Yeah, I think we should call her bluff this time. We're her parents. She cannot fool us all the time."

"It's okay, Sudha, let's give her one last chance. I don't want her to be upset."

"Okay. Last time, Naren. We cannot keep spoiling her."

"I promise."

They went to Harsha's room and opened the door slightly to watch her sleep peacefully. She had a round face and curly hair. A few strands of hair fell on her face as the fan continued to rotate at maximum pace. She looked so much like Sudha. The curly hair and the oval face.

Naren, on the other hand, had a mango-shaped face and sharp features. Harsha had the naughtiest look on her face, but when she slept, she looked like an angel, just like Naren.

Her parents stood for a few minutes to adore her. Her room was filled with toys and dolls. There was a huge teddy bear on one side of her bed. There was a small library in the corner, with all her favourite books. The room was painted red, which was her favourite colour. Behind her bed, the wall had stickers of her favourite cartoon, Handy Manny. There was a wooden bench and a study table in front of the window on the right and a white glass cupboard next to her bathroom.

"I don't know any kid her age who has so many toys and a big room like this," said Sudha.

"Our girl deserves the best of everything."

"This reminds me, her birthday is coming up next month."

"Let's throw her a grand party. She's going to be ten."

Harsha's birthday was a monumental affair. They threw a surprise party at home for her friends, and then Naren treated their family at the Radisson Blu Plaza Hotel, Mysore.

"Naren and Sudha always go overboard pampering Harsha. It sets a high standard for us," Naren's brother complained, as everyone laughed.

"Well, Harsha looks lovely in her yellow frock," said Naren's mother.

"She's a complete reflection of her parents," added Sudha's mother.

A couple of days later, when Sudha was busy in the kitchen cooking, her phone rang. It was Harsha's teacher.

"Please come to the school immediately."

"Is Harsha alright?"

"Yes, please come soon."

Sudha was seated in front of the principal in her office.

"Please tell me what happened. I'm worried," said Sudha anxiously.

Harsha's teacher escorted a girl of Harsha's age into the principal's office. There was a blue bruise around the girl's left eye.

"Look, Mrs Sudha. This is your daughter's doing," the principal said.

"What? Harshika would never do that."

"Mrs Sudha, I am sorry to say this, but this is my last warning to you. Your daughter is the most disobedient girl in class. Her grades are bad. She misses most of the tests, always talks back to teachers, and now this."

"I would like to apologise to you on behalf of my daughter. I understand that she can be a little difficult sometimes, but I'm sure she would never punch anyone without a reason."

"I don't care about the reasons. Please take her home right now. If this happens again, I'm afraid you'll have to find another school for her."

"I'm really sorry; we will talk to her tonight. We'll make sure this never happens again," Sudha said and got up from her seat. She was about to leave when she saw the poor girl's bruised face. Her lip was beginning to swell now.

"I'm very sorry, *Beta*. I'm apologising to you from Harshika's side. Here is a bar of chocolate for you as a sorry from my side." She pulled a Dairy Milk from her purse and left.

Harsha was standing outside the Principal's office.

Sudha dragged her through the corridor and took her home. She didn't say a word on the way back as she was too furious to talk.

"*Pappa* and I will talk about this with you once he's back from work," she said, as they reached home.

When Naren came home, he was taken aback to see the atmosphere at home so sullen. It was Sudha who had opened the door for him. Harsha always ran to open the door for him and he'd pick her up, and then the narrations of the day would start. She would tell him everything that happened during her day. But today she was nowhere in sight..

"Where's she?"

"In her room."

"What happened?"

"Please freshen up. We'll talk after that."

Sudha narrated the incident to Naren in their room.

He did not seem perturbed at all. "I'm sure she had a reason."

"Naren, you didn't see that girl's face. Her face was blue, and her lips were swollen. I think we're spoiling her. She is out of control. This has to stop right now."

"Of course, I will not support her in this, but there has to be a reason for it."

"I felt so embarrassed in front of her principal and teacher today. I cannot be the mother who raised her kid like this."

"Let's talk to her and find out why she did it."

Harsha was sitting quietly in her room, playing a video game. The minute she saw her *pappa*, she began weeping.

"*Pappa*, please don't be angry."

"You were quiet all day. Why the tears when *pappa* is around?" said Sudha, which made Harsha cry even louder.

"Harsha, we're not angry, *Beta*. We just want to know why you beat the poor girl today," said Naren.

"It wasn't just me. She scratched my neck too." Harsha pointed to small red lines on her neck.

"Who started it, and why?" asked Sudha.

"She said I did not look as good as my parents, and I wouldn't even look moderately pretty as my *mamma* when I grew up. She said I look different from you. So I got angry and slapped her. Then she scratched me and I punched her in the face. She started screaming, and the teacher saw me beating her so they took me to the principal."

"See, I told you she wouldn't do it without a reason," Naren said to Sudha. To Harsha, he said, "*Beta*, this isn't right. You can't go around slapping people."

"But she hurt my feelings. You know how I always want to look like *mamma* when I grow up. She's so pretty."

"You are prettier than me, Baby. Promise me this won't happen again" said Sudha.

"Promise."

"Now go to bed," said Naren as he tucked her into bed. "Good night."

That academic year ended with Harsha getting the lowest grades in class. Her teacher told Sudha to send her for tuitions during the vacations. That night, Sudha expressed her concerns to Naren.

"She's still in middle school. She doesn't need tuitions," said Naren.

"But, Naren, her grades are the worst in class."

"Performance and grades in school don't mean a thing. She can do so much better in life. She's a smart girl."

"You should have come to school with me today. The teacher humiliated me in front of all the other parents. She said Harsha was extremely undisciplined and the worst performer in class."

"How dare she say that! We'll change her school if required. I'm not sending her for tuitions, she doesn't need them."

"Naren, we're spoiling her. There needs to be a line drawn somewhere."

"Okay, we can do one thing; you take her tuitions at home every day."

"I help her with her studies every day but she's not afraid of me. She needs a strict tutor."

"I will talk to her. I'll tell her that if she doesn't study with you, she'll have to go for tuition classes."

"Okay," said Sudha reluctantly.

Harshika didn't care about studies. She hated school. What she loved was playing video games, watching cartoons, and going out to play with her friends. She didn't like being asked what to do by others, thus she hated her teachers. At home, her parents never scolded her for anything. She did whatever she liked. They never pressurized her to eat or drink anything she didn't like. Whenever she wanted ice cream, they took her for ice cream. Every time she for craved chocolate cake, her *mamma* baked it for her. She could have any toys or books she wanted. She had never heard a "no" from them. Her cousins and friends also listened to everything she said; she was the leader of their group. But her teachers were driving her nuts. The evening tuitions were a pain. Her *pappa* had told her she had to join actual tuitions if she didn't obey her *mamma*. Therefore, she had to pretend to study well.

One fine day when Sudha was teaching Harsha, she stumbled upon a math sum that wasn't clearly explained in the book. So she started looking online for help. "Google is helpful sometimes."

"Yes, even my friends use it for studying," Harsha said. "Some of the apps are really helpful."

"Oh! There are learning apps as well?"

"Yes, *Mamma*. Why else do you think they perform so well? No one understands a word our teacher teaches."

"Is it? Why didn't you say something earlier? Do you want me to download the apps for you?"

"I need it every time I study. Also, whenever I go out to play with my friends and for my swimming classes, you and *pappa* worry about me so I was thinking, how about I have my own phone?"

"*Hmm*. Let me think about it."

The next day during breakfast, Sudha told Harsha that Naren had also agreed and they would buy her a phone.

"*Pappa* and I have discussed and we are okay to buy you a phone but you have to wait till your birthday."

"When shall we go shopping then?"

"*Pappa* and I will select the phone and gift it to you on your birthday."

"I want an Apple iPhone 8 Plus," said Harsha with shining eyes.

"We were thinking of something more basic. Besides, Apple phones are very expensive."

"Most of my friends have it. I want it too."

"Harsha, we cannot afford such an expensive phone. Your *pappa* and I also use the most basic models. You know that we only have a single income in this house. We give you the best of everything. This is too much for us."

"I want an iPhone only," shouted Harsha, banging her fists on the table.

"Your friends study well and get good grades. Do you ever compare that?"

"They study from their phones."

"The apps are the same for all phones. You're an absolute spoilt brat. We need to put an end to this. You're not getting a phone."

Harsha shoved the plate across the table, jumped to her feet, and ran to her room.

"Let's get her the phone she wants," said Naren that night when Sudha told him that she hadn't eaten lunch and was refusing to eat dinner as well.

"But, Naren, we cannot afford it. Her school fees, swimming and piano classes, and the household expenses—we are barely making our ends meet."

"We'll manage somehow."

"We are spoiling her."

"We just have one daughter and her happiness is more important. What would we have done without her? What are we going to do with all our savings if not spend on her?"

Sudha knew that her husband always gave in to their daughter's tantrums, no matter what she did, and ultimately Harsha would have get her way. There was no point in arguing with Naren. Besides, she was also worried that Harsha would go to bed hungry. So they both went to Harsha's room with her dinner plate.

"Get up Harsha, we're getting you your iPhone for your birthday," said Naren.

"C'mon now! I've made your favourite mac and cheese, please eat. You have not eaten anything since breakfast," said Sudha, as she sat on her bed and began to feed her.

Harsha was very happy that night. She had managed to get her favourite phone finally. She could flaunt it to all her friends now. She'd lied to her parents about her friends having iPhones. Most of them didn't even have a phone. That night, she dreamt of all the features it would have, and how easy her life would be after having the phone.

Her birthday finally arrived. Her parents were occupied with the party preparations. She could not wait to receive the gift in the evening. She wanted to have a look at it now. Her *mamma* was cooking snacks for the evening party, and her *pappa* was busy with the decorations. She tiptoed to their bedroom. Her parents' room was a simple room, painted in light blue, with a bed at the center of the room, and two light brown wooden cupboards on one side. They had two nightstands on each side of a bed, and a table and chair, which was next to the attached bathroom. She began to look for her new phone but couldn't find it anywhere. It was neither on their night stands nor their cupboards. She finally decided to open her *mamma's* safe in her cupboard where *mamma* kept her jewellery. She knew the hiding place of the key.

The phone wasn't there either. Frustrated, she kicked the locker door; a bundle of cash fell out. When she bent down to pick it up, she found a stack of papers under the bundle.

"Why are there papers in the locker?" she thought and skimmed through them.

Little did she know about the shock that would strike her like a lightning bolt and change her life forever! She felt a sudden darkness in front of her eyes. Her heart began to race, her mouth was running dry as she felt sudden shortness of breath. She walked to the living room with shaking legs and trembling hands holding the papers.

"Is the birthday girl all set for her party today?" asked Naren.

"*Mamma*!" Harsha shouted. "*Mamma*!"

"What happened, *Beta*?" Sudha asked as she walked into the living room.

"What is this?" Harsha waved the papers at them.

"Where did you get this?" asked Sudha, shaking.

"How could you hide something like this from me?" Tears began to roll down her cheeks.

"We were going to tell you when you were old enough to understand," said Sudha.

"I'm already eleven!"

"The papers don't mean anything. You are our daughter, Harsha." Sudha began to weep.

"This means I'm not your daughter. I'm just an unwanted girl who was picked up piteously by you. My friend at school was right, I'm not pretty like you, *Mamma*. Now I know the reason."

"No, no, that's not true. Naren, please say something." Sudha fell on the couch and shook Naren.

Naren was frozen.

"I can't believe all this while, I was such an ungrateful girl who kept troubling you for little things. I deserved to be abandoned. I don't deserve anything good. I don't want the phone. I don't want the party. I don't want anything." Harsha ran to her room and shut the door.

Sudha knocked on the door frenziedly, but she wouldn't open it. Giving up, she went back to the living room and sat next to Naren.

"It's our fault. We should have told her earlier," said Naren, finally breaking his silence.

"We kept procrastinating. We thought she wasn't ready, but frankly, I think it was us."

"Let us give her some time to process it. She will open the door in a while, I'm sure."

After an hour, Harsha finally opened the door. She was sitting cross-legged on a bench, holding her favourite doll in her hand, staring at the sky outside the window.

"We love you, Harsha. You are our child," said Naren warmly as both sat facing Harsha.

Harsha refused to look at them.

"We adopted you from an orphanage in town. But you weren't abandoned; your parents had died when you were about a month old, therefore a neighbour had taken you to this orphanage. We did not pick you out of pity, we were desperate for a child and we weren't able to have one. The moment we saw you, your *mamma* and I knew you were our child."

"The twinkle in your eyes when you saw us," Sudha said wiping her tears. "That is something I cannot forget, Harsha. It's not just us choosing you. You chose us as well, *Beta*."

"Why couldn't you tell me this earlier?" demanded Harsha as she turned to face them with anger and grief in her puffy eyes due to the crying.

"We tried to, but we weren't ready and kept delaying the conversation. As years passed, we forgot about the adoption. We started believing that you were our own. When you brought out the papers, we were shocked. We love you so much!" Naren reached over to give her a hug.

She shrank.

"Please," Sudha said. "Never doubt our love for you." Her voice trembled.

"Please forgive us. This wasn't fair to you. Take this birthday gift as a sorry from our side," said Naren, holding out the iPhone to her.

"I don't want it," said Harsha. She refused to look at the phone.

"Please, Harsha. You are our daughter. Those papers don't mean anything. You are ours. Just because our blood doesn't run in your veins doesn't mean you aren't our daughter. Some relationships are above blood and flesh."

"I have troubled you so much. I'm such a spoilt girl. You have given me everything, but I've always wanted more. I've never had any gratitude for anything. I'm sorry for having been such a selfish girl."

"You are supposed to be like this, Harsha. Like a child. Besides, you have never troubled us. We love you beyond words," said Sudha.

"I will try to be a better daughter. Somebody who should be grateful to you for changing her fate."

"Harsha, we love you as you are. It's your right to demand anything you want. We are your parents. It's our duty."

"No, it's not."

"We will give you some time to accept it. We want our cheerful girl back in the evening. You are the apple of our eye."

With those words, Naren and Sudha left to continue the party preparations.

Harsha stared at the gift wrapped in white gift paper with cartoons on it. It was wrapped in a red ribbon with a label addressed as:

To our dear Harsha,
We love you; Hope this gift makes you happy. ☺
Happy Birthday!
From,
Mamma & Pappa.

She felt ashamed for throwing tantrums for a phone she didn't deserve. She remembered all her other fits, and how her parents had made sure she got what she wanted. The numerous sacrifices they'd made for her sake. Her *mamma* had not bought herself a saree for ages now. She was always dressed in faded old cotton sarees that had shrunk at the bottom. The gowns she wore at home were equally dull. She neither wore make-up nor went to salons. Her *pappa* always wore the same white shirt to work, the one that had a torn, discoloured collar while Harsha had a cupboard full of new clothes and got expensive haircuts. Her friends had to borrow books from a library, but Harsha had a library at home. They got toys only on birthdays, but Harsha got them every time she asked for it.

Her parents had forgone so much for her sake. She remembered how her grandmother had forced her *mamma* to at least buy a saree on Diwali, but she'd refused, saying that she didn't need it. Her parents' room was old and had paint peeling off everywhere, but Harsha's room was expensively decorated. Had she failed to notice all of this? Or was it that she didn't care enough? It was time to put an end to the over-pampering. She was too ashamed of herself to even look in the mirror.

She finally washed her face and got ready for the party. She wasn't going to bother her parents anymore. They'd already done enough for her.

She entered the living room. It was decorated with her favourite red colour balloons, and a golden Happy Birthday banner hung behind the table that had a red velvet flavoured cake on it. Everyone began singing the "Happy Birthday" song loudly as soon as they saw her. Her parents smiled at her sweetly. She refused to look at them directly, still mad.

After the cake cutting was over, her *mamma* served everyone potato chips, a pizza slice, a pastry and, a glass of coke. Her friends surrounded her and began to compliment her. She looked pretty, dressed in a light pink chiffon frock. Her pink star earrings and hairband matched her dress. They also complimented her *mamma* for her delicious homemade pizza. Sudha specialised in cooking children's snacks. She had won cooking competitions at school numerous times for her mac and cheese, chocolate lava cake, and pizzas.

"You are so lucky, Harsha. Your *mamma* makes such lovely items," said her friend Shruti, licking her fingers.

"Yes," agreed another friend, Ramya.

"Harsha, why don't you show them your birthday gift?" said Sudha as she served them more slices of pizza.

"Okay," said Harsha hesitantly and went to her room.

Her friends followed her.

"Wow, I wish I'd an iPhone too. My parents promised me a cycle if I got 90%, but I missed it by one percent," said Dilip.

After the party was over, and Harsha had gone to bed, Sudha shared her anxiety with Naren. "She's too quiet. And her iPhone is untouched."

"Don't worry, Sudha. She will take a couple of days to recover," Naren consoled her.

The next few weeks were very difficult for Sudha and Naren. Harsha studied well and acted like an adult. She obeyed them. She made no demands and ate whatever she was offered. Once school began, she went quietly, without her usual tantrums.

Her teachers saw Harsha turn over a new leaf. During the parent-teacher meet, her teachers told Sudha that they were very happy with Harsha's behaviour.

But instead of being happy, Sudha was more worried. "She has completely changed. I want my daughter back, Naren," she said to Naren one night.

"I miss her too. She doesn't come and greet me after work anymore. She's like a complete robot that obeys us and does whatever she's been asked to," said Naren.

"Should we talk to her again? I miss her tantrums. I'm probably the first mother in the world to say this."

"We have spoken to her so many times, Sudha. You remember how she lashed out last time saying that we need to stop making more sacrifices for her as we have already done her a favour by adopting her. She accused us of having given up our whole life to fulfil all her demands."

Harsha overheard her parents' conversation from her room and was puzzled. She'd thought that her turning into a new person would make her parents happy. They would have no teacher complaints; they could spend more on themselves. But they seemed to be getting uneasy. They worried about her all the time. They'd even reduced their social meets with friends. She wondered where she'd gone wrong. All she wanted was for her parents to be happy with adopting the girl they'd rescued.

The next day, while going to school, Harsha's eyes fell on their family photo in the living room showcase. It was a picture taken on her last birthday. They all looked so happy together. Things had changed so much this year. Last year she was such a happy-go-lucky girl. Everyone at the party had agreed that Harsha was a complete fusion of her parents' looks.

"How wrong were they! Why did everyone give such fake compliments?" she thought.

That evening she decided to go through their family photos. She wanted to compare and see how different she looked from her parents. She saw a hundred of photos of her baby self. Her *pappa* had clicked her pictures from all angles in all poses. Then she started to skim through her parents' wedding photos. Her *pappa* looked so handsome, and her *mamma* looked so pretty! Harsha wished she was as half as pretty as her. She then started going through their honeymoon pictures, and their anniversary photos year after year. They looked very young and had relaxed faces. But something seemed to be missing in their eyes.

The next set of pictures were after Harsha was born. They had taken her on a vacation to South India. Something was different in their eyes as compared to the anniversary photos.

Harsha couldn't sleep that night. She tossed and turned for hours before she finally accepted it to herself! It was her. She was what was missing from their life. She was wrong about her being a burden to them. It wasn't just they who had rescued her from the orphanage; she had also rescued them from their loneliness. She'd completed their family.

The others weren't wrong about her looking like the mirror image of her parents. She did resemble them. They'd raised her to be like them. That meant that she was a reflection of them. She did resemble her *mamma* after all. She would grow up and be as pretty as her.

She then began to realize how bored her parents were every time she went on school trips or visited her grandparents. They had no life without her. Lately, her *pappa* seemed low since she'd stopped greeting him after work. Her *mamma* sat in the living room, bored in the evenings since Harsha had stopped making demands for new food items. Their life bore no meaning without her.

The next day at breakfast, Harsha began to play a game on her new phone. Her parents smiled at each other. Harsha had finally started using the iPhone.

"*Mamma*, I don't like *upma*. Please make something else for me," she demanded.

Sudha's joy knew no bounds. Her daughter was back. She rushed to the kitchen to make her a cheese sandwich.

"*Pappa*, I need some new books to read, I'm bored with all the books in the library," she said.

"Anything for you, Harsha. We'll go shopping today," he said.

"Do you know the meaning of your name, Harshika?" he asked Harsha as Sudha came out of the kitchen with Harsha's cheese sandwich.

"No."

"It means 'happiness.'" He smiled at Sudha and her.

"You have brought happiness into our lives, Harsha," said Sudha, hugging her tightly with moist eyes.

"Speaking of happiness, you know what would make me happy?" asked Harsha.

"What?" asked both of them in chorus?

"If you'd allow me to re-decorate your room" smiled Harsha.

BEING "NORMAL"

"**O**ut!" cried the yellow team in unison, as Rohan walked out of the playground.

His team members frowned at him in annoyance. He heard them discuss amongst themselves as he took his helmet off.

"He has not crossed twenty runs in any match. Today was the worst. A zero! Why would you keep a player like that in our team?" he heard someone ask.

"I can't help it. Rohan's father is the chairman of our society. He does the majority of funding for our cricket matches. If I don't take Rohan on the team, we won't be having any sports events," his captain answered.

This was it! Rohan was tired of *pai* running everything for him. He started to rush home, fuming.

Mai hurried behind him. "Rohan, it's just a match. Don't be upset."

"It's not about the match, *Mai*," he said over his shoulder. "*Pai* always does that! He bullies everyone. *Mhojem Khaim self-respect na*. I refuse to fall prey to his bullying. I've told you a million times that I hate cricket. I'm done."

He ran home. *Mai*, who couldn't chase him, returned to the playground to call his *pai*.

Enraged, Rohan paced in his room. He was frightened of his *pai* and did whatever was asked of him. On the other hand, his *vodlo bhaav* Ravi did whatever he wanted to without being dictated by their *pai*. Rohan wished he could be more like him. But today he was finally going to stand up for himself. He threw his bat out of the window.

Rohan lived in Panjim in North Goa with his parents and elder brother, Ravi. Their house was a very old property built during the Portuguese invasion of Goa. It was a villa that had a small veranda in front with some cane furniture. Multiple pillars held up the building on the front side. The living room had plastered tiles with a square design on each tile. There were two bedrooms on each side of the hall. The kitchen was right in front of the living room. The villa had a small lawn on the left side which had begun to dry up in the scorching heat; the roses and hibiscus flowers surrounding the garden had withered too. The house was on a single floor but had a terrace above that gave a beautiful view of Miramar beach.

Rohan was a shy guy by nature. He had jet black hair and coal-black eyes. He looked extremely handsome, like his *pai*. Ravi on the other hand had inherited their *mai's* big features. Both brothers were tall, but Rohan had a slouchy body whereas Ravi was fit who exercised regularly.

"Why was the bat thrown out of the window, Rohan?" *Pai* tossed the bat back on the sofa.

"I'm done with cricket."

"Just because you made no runs today?"

"No, *Pai*. I'm done trying to please you. You forced my team to take me on. I'm not even good enough for gully cricket. It's not my sport."

"You know I don't take 'no' for an answer, Rohan. You cannot just drop out of the game. I've spent so much money on your years of coaching."

"I didn't ask you to!"

"Rohan, please don't talk to your *pai* like that. If you don't want to play cricket, it's okay. You can choose any other sport," *mai* said.

"I don't want to play any sport. I don't like sports," shouted Rohan in frustration.

"So, what do you like? Playing your guitar in the room all the time? Which youngster locks himself in a room all day? Be a man like your *bhaav*, Rohan. Look how he's selected for state-level cricket from Goa. I couldn't be more proud of him," *Pai* said.

"Please continue being proud of him. I will leave the house once college is over. Then you'll be happy." Tears began to roll down his cheeks.

"Stop crying," *pai* said. "Don't be such a girl."

"I'm not crying. I'm just mad."

Rohan slammed the door to his room shut and grabbed his guitar. He was one of the best guitar players in college. But his parents failed to recognise his talent. They wanted their sons to prove their manhood by playing sports. What sort of logic was that?

As he strummed the guitar, he began to compose a new song. He started to hum:

Unfamiliar to the bizarre world,
Lost in crowds of prejudiced beliefs,
Struggling to create his identity,
Fraught to prove himself,
A guy who once lived!
But the judgmental minds continue to stare him in the eye...

A knock on the door interrupted him. It was Ravi.

"*Mai* told me you had a fight with *pai* and quit cricket."

"Yes, I did, *Irmao.*"

"I'm proud of you, Rohan. You stood up for yourself. Finally." Ravi began to clap.

"Yes, I took inspiration from you. Step by step, I'm going to finally get what I want."

"My case is different. I hope you know that you're never going to be able to convince them."

"I know that."

"Promise me you won't do anything stupid while I'm gone, okay?"

"Where are you going?"

"To Mumbai, for my matches, and then a weekend trip with my girlfriend to Lonavala." He winked.

"You're just twenty-four! How did she agree to go out with you? Isn't she like twenty-eight or something?"

"It's my charm." Quickly packing a bag, he left.

Rohan dialled Sarah's number.

"Hi, Rohan, what's up?"

"Let's meet for a beer tonight."

"Done. Same place?"

"Of course."

Rohan smiled to himself. Sarah was always there for him, no matter what. He remembered how he'd met her on the first day of college. Rohan had come late to class, dressed in a printed shirt and tight pants. The professor had made a joke about his attire, at which the class had laughed. Except for Sarah. She offered him a seat beside her and said that she had loved his dressing style. From that day on, they were together always.

She was seated at the bar at Café Mojo, sipping her draught beer when Rohan entered.

Sarah was a short girl who had a slim figure and was always referred to as petite by the girls in their college. She had beautiful brown eyes and high cheekbones. She had a gorgeous smile and flawless white skin. She had shoulder-length hair and always left it open wearing a red velvet hairband. She always dressed up in shorts and t-shirts or jumpsuits and carried a backpack wherever she went.

"Sorry, I'm late."

"Tell me something new, Rohan."

"I said I'm sorry."

"Fine. Sit. What's up?"

He signalled to the bartender for his usual beer and turned to her.

"My mind is fucked, man." He narrated the cricket incident to her in detail.

"You finally stood up for yourself after nineteen years. Wow!" She patted his back.

"I've got a long way to go."

"Baby steps, one at a time."

"Why do they always have football matches on the screens in bars?" asked Rohan irritably.

"Because guys love watching it, guys unlike you, who are 'normal' and love sports," she teased.

"Let's get out of here." He nudged her.

"Wait, let me finish my beer." She gulped down her beer and followed him out.

They rode to Miramar beach on Rohan's bike.

At the beach, Sarah asked, "Now what? You're going to play your guitar here?"

"Yes, I've composed half a song. Want to show it to my girlfriend." He winked.

"Rohan, I hope you'll be able to tell your parents about us very soon."

"Not even close to ready," he said in dismay.

They spent an hour at the beach and then had an elaborate dinner of chili prawns, chicken tikka, rice, and fish curry at an eatery near the beach.

That night Rohan could not sleep. *Pai* refused to even look at him.

Mai had tried her best to make Rohan feel better about the morning's incident. She had come to his room that night and explained to him *pai*'s point of view. "You know how everyone is constantly comparing you both with your *pai*. He was a state-level cricket player and very well-known, so he wants the same appreciation for you both."

"But, *Mai*, I play the guitar in cafes and bars."

"That's nowhere close to a career. If you don't want to play sports, that's okay. But at least make a decent career."

"*Pai* wasted his life trying to be a national-level cricket player. If he didn't have his bike-renting business, he would not be able to make a decent living. The sports field isn't easy to be successful in."

"Yes, I know, *Bai*. He wanted at least one of his sons to fulfil his dream of being a national-level cricketer. But, today, I've understood that you hate it. But please try making a decent career in something. Mr Gonsalves commented that you don't mix with youngsters during social gatherings and are always locked up in the room, like a girl. Your *pai* was hurt to know that our neighbours are gossiping about you like this. That's why he kept pushing you more for cricket."

"Who are they to judge me, *Mai*?"

"I know they aren't, but when everyone around comments on you saying that you're not manly, like your *pai* and Ravi, he gets upset."

"I'm not going to play sports just to prove my manhood. And regarding my career, I love music, so I'm not going to give up on it. Music doesn't make anyone feminine."

"Not music! They say your dressing isn't very..."

"Very what?"

"Nothing, go to sleep."

"No, what do people say, *Mai*?"

"The other day our neighbour, Mrs Shenoy, said that your dressing is feminine."

"What does she know about fashion? She's so old-fashioned. Ask her to mind her own business. Besides, gone are the days when men wore boring clothes. Now everyone likes to dress well. Men like me are called metrosexual. Please tell her."

"Metro... What?"

"Guys who like to dress well."

"Okay, *Bai*. Go to sleep. Goodnight."

Their conversation began to haunt him. He couldn't keep making excuses for his behaviour. He'd wait for *Irmao* to return home.

One night after dinner, when they all were seated in the living room, *pai* began, "Ravi, your coach says that you can be a national player if you practise well. I heard you were the 'Man of the Match.'"

"Yes, *Pai*."

"You make us very proud. On the other hand, look at your *dhakto bhaav*, Rohan. He refuses to play cricket, refuses to make a decent career, always stuck to his guitar. He doesn't even have friends in college."

Rohan glared at *pai*, but refused to say anything.

Pai continued, "He only hangs out with that girl, Sarah. I don't know what she sees in him to go out with someone so useless."

"She isn't my girlfriend." Rohan finally spoke.

"She was the only good thing in your life. And you broke up with her as well?"

"No, we did not break up! We never dated."

"Why did you lie to us then, Rohan?" *Mai* asked.

"Because you keep worrying about what people might say about me. Here's the truth that I've been keeping from you for years now." He took a deep breath, closing his eyes for a brief second, and finally said what he had always dreaded to say. He had imagined a million ways of how he would say it, and here was that moment he'd waited for. Finally came the words from his mouth, his lips trembling as he took shallow breaths from his mouth while saying it. "I'm gay!"

"Finally," murmured Ravi.

"What!" *Pai* looked like he had been punched in the stomach.

"What are you saying, Rohan?" *Mai* sounded dazed.

"I like boys, *Mai*," Rohan said quietly.

"Ravi did you know about this?"

"You'll have to accept me for who I am," said Rohan, trying to sound confident.

Thwack! *Mai* slapped him on the face.

"What are you doing, *Mai!*" Ravi pulled *mai* away from Rohan.

Pai, who'd frozen in shock, began to laugh. "This is such a joke, Rohan. No son of mine can be like this. Someone has brainwashed you into all this crap. All that western culture is getting to you."

"This is not a joke, *Pai*," protested Rohan.

He turned on his wife. "You are partly responsible for this. Supporting him always in everything. If you'd listened to me and put him in sports, all this feminine behaviour would have disappeared. He doesn't even have male friends. Once he graduates, I'm going to talk to Sarah's *pai* and get them married."

"I cannot marry her. It would ruin her life. I like boys, *pai*. Please try to understand me."

"Understand you?" *Pai* grabbed the bat from the corner and began to beat him. *Mai* and Ravi looking in horror for a second. Then *mai* ran to Rohan, trying to cover him. But *Pai* didn't stop at that. He trying to push her away and continued beating Rohan.

"*Pai*, no!" said Rohan as he screamed in pain.

Ravi finally managed to drag both his parents away into their room.

From the living room, Rohan could hear their outrage. He was shaking now.

Ravi returned, wrapped an arm around Rohan's shoulders, and helped him to their room. There were bruises on forearms and thighs, most of the areas had turned blue and some parts of his skin had cuts from which his flesh peeked. As soon as Ravi noticed the wounds, he began to apply Dettol on them. Neither of them said a word.

Rohan lay on his bed thinking about his childhood, his teens, the day he'd finally come out to his *bhaav*.

He was thirteen, and they'd been on a school picnic. On the bus, the guys in his class were talking about their first crush.

"Rohan, don't you like any girl at school?" his friend Samuel asked.

"I just haven't found anyone yet."

Arun said, "I'm going to the waterfall with Anita tonight, don't disturb me, okay guys? I've been wanting to know if she likes me. Today is the day I'm going to finally find out."

Rohan had a deep liking for Arun, he just didn't know what kind it was. All he knew was that he'd never felt that way about any pretty girl as he felt about Arun. He always felt a spark; a jolt of electricity running through his body every time he saw Arun.

Arun was the most confident guy Rohan knew; he wasn't bothered about pleasing anybody. Rohan always watched him during swimming classes. Arun's body was a perfectly carved figure of a teenager destined to become a handsome man. Rohan didn't understand why he felt that way about a guy. He'd heard about homosexual people. Was this what being gay meant? He wasn't sure yet. He had googled and found out that his feelings resembled a homosexual person's, but it was too early to conclude anything.

That day after lunch, Rohan saw Arun standing alone near the waterfall. He had never seen him so low. He decided to go and speak to him.

"What happened Arun?"

"She rejected me, man."

"Oh. Anita! Don't worry. There are plenty of girls out there," said Rohan, patting Arun's hand.

Arun smiled and looked Rohan in the eye.

Did Arun feel the same about him as he did? Rohan wondered. This was his chance to find out. He was standing very close to Arun now. He could smell the other boy's musky cologne. It all happened so fast that Rohan's brain got fuzzy. He threw his arms around him.

"Hey, it's okay, man. I'm fine," said Arun, patting his back.

Rohan began to get closer to Arun's face and was about to kiss him on the lips when Arun pushed him away. Rohan fell to the ground.

"What the hell was that, Rohan?"

Rohan looked up to see his classmates surrounding them. Everyone was looking at him in disgust. He got to his feet.

"*Eww.* Rohan is so disgusting."

"We boys should stay away from him."

"Boys' molester," he heard someone murmur.

Nobody talked to Rohan for the rest of the day. On the way back home, he sat alone in the school bus. After that incident, everyone in school nicknamed him "Boys' molester." He spent his next two years completely isolated. During lunch breaks, he sat alone. When he was fifteen, he finally decided to speak to Ravi.

"*Irmao*, I need to tell you something."

"What?" Ravi asked casually.

"This is serious, Ravi. Please pay attention."

"What did you do? Kill someone?"

"No, no! I think I like boys."

"What?"

"Yes, I think I'm homosexual."

"Dude, are you out of your mind? This is absurd. I know you are a normal guy."

"I don't feel attracted to women. I like boys. I find them attractive. I don't know who I can talk to about this. At school, nobody talks to me because of an incident that happened two years ago."

"What incident?"

"I tried to kiss a guy."

"*Eww.* I heard about this in school but thought it was just a rumour," said Ravi.

"It's true."

"You'll get over it. I think you're watching too many Hollywood movies. Once you go to college and see girls in short skirts, you'll forget everything."

Ravi was wrong. Rohan wasn't into girls at all. He hated hanging out with guys; all they talked about was sports and girls. He didn't like how they disrespected girls, and only talked about their bodies. They were also mean to him and made fun of the way he dressed. The only girl's company he enjoyed was Sarah's. He shared everything with her.

To cover up Rohan's queerness, they did not stop rumours about them dating. His parents were also happy about this. They were convinced that Rohan was normal despite his "absurd" dressing sense, and "feminine" behaviour as they called it.

An incident during Rohan's college days had changed Ravi's thoughts about Rohan. Somebody in the neighbourhood who knew about Rohan's crush on Arun in school started texting him, pretending to be Arun. He apologised to Rohan and said that he had been too scared in school, and felt the same way about Rohan. The texting continued for weeks, and finally, he asked Rohan to meet him at Café Coffee Day.

Rohan was overjoyed.

Arun also asked him to dress up in his white flowery shirt and maroon pants. When he reached the place, he saw that guys from his neighbourhood were waiting for him at the parking lot. When they saw him, they began to laugh.

"We fooled you, Rohan. Look at you, all dressed up," said one.

"I love your shirt and pink pants," shouted another.

"Boys' molester, no one likes you." They laughed and hi-fived one another.

Rohan was humiliated. His face began to turn red from distress.

Ravi, who happened to be at the same café, was leaving with his friends around that time. Spotting Rohan, he asked him the matter.

Rohan narrated the matter between sobs.

"This is the first and last time anyone harasses my *bhaav*. If anything happens to him again, or if anyone says a word, there's going to a lot of bones cracking," Ravi said in a threatening tone as he walked toward the boys.

"Who messaged Rohan?" he asked in a loud voice.

Nobody responded.

"If you don't hand over the person, Ravi will be beating up everyone," said one of Ravi's friends.

The crowd pointed fingers at Kevin, who was Mrs Gonsalves' son. She was the nosiest lady in the neighbourhood and loved to feed on gossip, but wasn't aware of her own son's mischiefs. This wasn't his first prank. He'd done a lot of others in the past with some girls and guys.

Ravi punched him hard in the stomach. His friends encircled the group and began to hit the other guys.

"Ravi, please stop it," shouted Rohan in embarrassment.

Ravi walked backward, looking Kevin in the eye. "Last warning," he said, and left.

On the way back Rohan began, "I'm not a damsel in distress, Ravi. I don't need my *bhaav* to rescue me."

"But they were humiliating you. Nobody gets to do that to my *bhaav.*"

"You are a real don, I swear. The way you threatened them, it was so funny to see their scared faces." Rohan started laughing as his anger cooled down.

"Don't you know? I'm a don at college. Everyone is frightened of me."

"You're so cool, *Irmao*. Wish I was brave like you."

"I'm sorry for making fun of you in the past. I'm not fully convinced about this homosexuality of yours. But from now, I will not mock you."

"Thanks, *Irmao.*"

"But you should know that *mai* and *pai* will never, ever accept it. They'll guilt you into marrying a girl. And society will never accept you. You will have to compromise, Rohan."

Compromise, Rohan. Compromise, Rohan. Compromise, Rohan.

The words echoed in his ears as he sat in bed recollecting the past. Ravi was right. Nobody was ever going to accept him. He went to bed, deeply unhappy.

The next day *mai* broke the silence at the breakfast table. "Rohan, be home early today. I've taken an appointment at 5 pm with Renee *pachhi* for you."

"Good idea, let her drill some sense into this idiot." *Pai* glared at him.

Rohan ate his breakfast of *usal pav* quietly. He picked up his bag and went to college without a word.

"*Mai* wants to take me to meet my *pachhi*, who's a psychiatrist," he told Sarah after he had narrated yesterday's happenings to her.

"Maybe this is a good thing. You know that she's highly educated and has always been a loving aunt. She might actually support you in this."

"My family isn't really modern, Sarah. I know I'm going to have to compromise in my life. They will get me married to a girl in a few years. In fact, my *pai* said he's going to get me married to you."

"*Haha*, that's funny. Besides, you know what, Aaron has finally started to text me. He's also doing some light flirting. Things might be progressing. Fingers crossed." She blushed.

"Finally, Sarah! After years of stalking, you're finally talking to him."

That evening Rohan and *mai* went to Renee *pachhi's* clinic. She was one of Rohan's favourite aunts, but now things were going to get complicated with her.

Rohan was called inside. His *mai* followed him in.

Renee was seated calmly in her chair. She smiled at both of them. "How are you doing, Rohan?" she asked warmly.

"Good," said Rohan in a low voice.

"Could you wait outside, Leila?" she turned to *mai*.

"I want to hear everything, and also help you in convincing him this is wrong," *mai* protested.

"He's my patient now. Please give us some privacy," Renee said firmly.

Mai left, muttering under her breath.

"So, Rohan, let us begin the session. Please tell me everything that has been bothering you, starting from your childhood. I'm your therapist now. Forget that I'm your *pachhi* for the time being. Be completely honest with me. Whatever we discuss here stays here."

Rohan narrated everything, starting with his confusion over his sexual identity from the time he was a child. He ended with the incident from last night.

"I'm so sorry that you have been going through so much. I'd no idea. Wish you'd spoken to me about this much earlier."

"I wasn't sure if anyone would ever accept it."

"You must understand that our generation is quite conservative. So I'm not surprised that it's difficult for your parents. Especially, for your *pai*, as you know very well."

"They want me to marry a girl."

"They will take a few years to accept it, Rohan. Don't expect a change overnight. Meanwhile, I will prescribe you anti-anxiety medicine. I want you to meet me weekly for an hour and talk about your feelings."

"What will you tell my parents, though? They want you to change me."

"You leave that to me. Don't speak about this matter to them for a couple of days. I will also ask them to leave you alone till you take your medicines. This will help you relax. For now, only focus on getting better. You have gone through so much since childhood."

The weekly sessions with Renee *pachhi* were a blessing. She'd become a friend to him, someone with whom he could share everything. He told her every incident that happened in college. He'd started to feel more and more confident about himself.

A couple of months passed. *Pai* raised the uncomfortable topic again. "So, Rohan, have you started feeling normal again? You've been seeing Renee *pachhi* for months now."

"Yes, I feel more confident about myself."

"So you're over the queerness now?"

"Not even close. I'm proud of being gay."

"What?" asked *pai* furiously, as he got up from the sofa. He then went to the kitchen to talk to Leila, muttering something to himself.

Rohan could hear him yelling at *mai*. "Your *bhoin* has done nothing. He's getting worse. Your whole family is useless," *pai* was shouting.

Rohan could hear *mai* sob.

Angry, he went to the kitchen. "*Pai*, there's no need to attack *mai*'s family like always. Renee *pachhi* is the only person who understands me."

"She's lost her mind. All these psychiatrists are useless. They only take money to waste others' time."

Mai wiped her tears with her gown. "Let me speak to Renee. We will have to stop your sessions, Rohan. It's not going anywhere."

"But I like talking to her. Her sessions are the only thing I look forward to all week."

"But what's the point? She has not done her job," said *mai*.

Mai went into her room, closing the door behind her.

Rohan put his ear to the door. He heard a "Hello." *Mai* must be calling Renee *pachhi*.

"But Renee," *Mai*'s voice said, "you were supposed to make him forget about all this nonsense." A few minutes of silence. "But... Hmm. I'm listening. Yes, but no." Then, "I'm sorry; we won't be able to send Rohan to you anymore." More silence from *mai*. "It's not just *bhouji*. I'm not convinced about this either." Then a final, "No, no, please promise me. Ok, bye."

Rohan was bitterly disappointed. Renee *pachhi* was the only one who could understand him, but he was forbidden from seeing her. He dialled her number. She disconnected it.

A few minutes later, she left him a message. "Sorry, Rohan. I cannot see you anymore. Leila has made me promise her that. I'm worried about you, so I'm sharing a number with you. Please get in touch with her. Her name is Rima, she will help you out."

Rohan was furious. He wondered why his *pachhi* had to be so sincere. She could have continued meeting him secretly. He was an adult now. After a couple of days, when his anger had finally cooled down, he dialled the number his *pachhi* had given him.

"Hi, is this Rima?"

"Yes, are you Rohan? I was expecting your call. I've saved your number."

"Yes, I am."

"Do you want to meet me at Sodi tonight? Say 7 pm?"

Rohan arrived at the venue sharp on time. He ordered a drink for himself, wondering why a psychiatrist would ask to meet him at a bar.

And after sometime, Rima came and sat beside him. He could recognise her through her WhatsApp display picture.

"Hi, Rohan." A woman came up to him.

"Hi, Rima." She seemed to be dressed in party clothes. He was confused. "Is this a party?"

"This is an LGBTQ party."

"What's that?"

"We have queer people like us here." She smiled.

"You mean you're gay too?"

"Bisexual, actually."

"What does that mean?"

"It means I'm both into men and women, Rohan."

"Oh!"

"So you're still new to the world, *huh*? When did you come out?"

"I was fifteen when I came out to my brother."

"I've been out since twelve."

"So, what are these parties like?"

"It's for people like us, Rohan. You'll find new friends who will understand you. Also, you'll meet someone special here, I'm sure."

"Really?" said Rohan, excited.

"Yes, let me introduce you to my friends."

Rima took him around, introducing him to her friends. "Hi guys, this is Rohan."

"Rohan, this is Paul, Antony, Laura, Keith, Tina, and Myra."

Rohan had never enjoyed so much in his life. He finally felt like he belonged. They played foosball and drank beer. They told stories of how they came out, and how their families took it.

"I was beaten up by the police when my neighbours complained about me," said Paul.

"*Mai* got me married. But after two years, I'm finally divorced and happy," said Myra.

"My parents have disowned me," announced Keith.

Rohan felt like his issues weren't as bad. He was beginning to see life from a different angle. For the first time in his life, he found hope. He messaged his *pachhi* that night, thanking her for introducing him to Rima. He'd found a new set of friends now. They started hanging out regularly. He found Paul particularly attractive. He was broad-shouldered, with deep black eyes, dark eyelashes, and jet-black hair. Rohan simply loved his attitude and the way he carried himself. But he never spoke about his feelings because he didn't want a repeat of the school incident again.

One day Paul messaged him on his personal chat. Usually, it was in their common WhatsApp group. Rohan's heart skipped a beat.

"Hi, Rohan. Do you want to meet tonight?"

"Hi. Yes, for sure," replied Rohan.

"Can we do dinner at Fisherman's Wharf?"

"Yep, who all are coming?"

"I was thinking, just you and me, Rohan."

Rohan's heart skipped a beat again. "Oh, okay. What time?"

"7 pm?"

"Cool, I'll see you there."

Rohan had dressed carefully that night. His previous experiences came to mind, but he ignored them. Paul looked very handsome in his dark blue shirt and jeans. He looked different and nervous.

"Hi, Rohan."

"Hi, Paul. What's up?"

"Shall we order?"

"Sure."

The dinner was extremely awkward. Both were quiet and didn't say much.

"Would you like to come home after dinner? We could do a movie," stuttered Paul.

"Why not?" said Rohan, trying to sound confident.

After dinner, Paul drove Rohan to his house. Paul went inside to get drinks while Rohan sat awkwardly on the couch.

Paul returned with the drinks and began to search for movies on Netflix. Rohan was aware of Paul's awkwardness. Nervous himself, he turned to Paul and kissed him. Paul responded immediately.

"That was amazing," said Paul as he took Rohan's arms leading him towards the bedroom.

They lay exhausted on the bed after their love-making. It was Rohan's first time. He had never known how it felt to be happy and be content. It wasn't just that, he also finally started to accept and embrace himself as a person. He didn't care about the world now. He could feel that it wasn't just him, but Paul was feeling the same. He could tell from the twinkle in his eyes and the way he was constantly smiling.

"My first time." Rohan was embarrassed.

"You don't say. You seemed confident," said Paul, blushing.

"Thanks. What about you?" Rohan was feeling proud now.

"My first time too."

"Why don't you stay with me tonight?"

"If you say so."

That night Rohan slept well for the first time in his life. He couldn't feel more normal. Someone wanted him, and that feeling was the best reward he could ever ask for. He had never felt more pleased in his life.

Rohan and Paul began to date thereafter. Rohan started to see his life differently. They were falling in love. He did not worry about answering to society, nor about how his *pai* would react if he heard about him having a boyfriend.

Rohan had never been in love before. Out of that love came a new song.

Unfamiliar to the bizarre world,
Lost in crowds of prejudice beliefs,
Struggling to create his identity,
Fraught to prove himself,
A guy who once lived!
But the judgmental minds continue to stare him in the eye…!
One day he walked in a different world
And finally found his kind of people!
That's the day he began to face the mirror.
He created his own identity.
He finally found himself
He is now so proud of himself with his newfound integrity
Whether he is accepted or not!

Rohan completed his graduation. It was time for the graduation ceremony. He decided to speak on stage for the first time in his life. He invited his parents, Renee *pachhi* and Ravi. His parents, who were very hesitant about coming, had to be dragged there by Ravi.

As Rohan stood on the stage with his cap and gown, everyone stared at him with judgment in their eyes.

Rohan began. "Hi, guys. I am here today on the stage with a lot of courage gathered over the years because of my friends, and especially my *pachhi's* help. I had a lot of convincing to do for my teachers and Principal to agree for this speech today because it is a childhood-to-college personal journey.

"First of all, I would like to announce that I shall continue playing my guitar at bars and cafes in Goa. Everyone has a right to choose their career. It should be your personal decision and there's no good and bad career, as some may phrase it. Anything done from the heart is a good choice. I was always an introvert and scared of people judging me, but today I've come out and can proudly say that I'm a homosexual who doesn't care about what everyone thinks. Yes, I'm so proudly saying it because section 377 was repealed last week. I now have a boyfriend, Paul, and we're going to be moving in together tomorrow. This wouldn't have been possible without my *pachhi's* support. My parents are probably going to hate her for the rest of their lives, but she has given me my life back. I would like to thank my *vodlo bhaav*, who never really understood the concept but never opposed my decisions and always protected me; my best friend Sarah, who never judged me and always stood by my side; my queer group, who were the best of friends I could have, and also because of whom I met Paul. I would also like to thank my parents for bringing me into this world and would like to tell them that I will always love them, whether they fully accept me or not. A special thanks to my college for giving me permission to be so open on stage. Happy Graduation to you all."

After Rohan finished his speech, he heard cheering and endless claps. Everyone tossed their caps up. A few people in the audience even stood up for him. None of the previous speeches got as much cheering as he did.

Rohan went home to say a final goodbye to his parents before he moved out.

"I'll miss you, *bhaav*," said Ravi as he was leaving.

He touched *pai's* and *mai's* feet. *Pai* continued to ignore him. *Mai* hugged him tightly. Rohan left home with a heavy heart and tears in his eyes.

Paul was waiting for him outside in his car.

"*Bidaai* done, Rohan?" he asked, laughing.

"Shut up," said Rohan, wiping his tears.

"Did your speech move your parents?"

"*Mai* has finally started to accept me but cannot say it out loud, is what I could sense. As for my *pai*, he still lives in denial."

"Both my parents live in denial, but life moves on," said Paul.

"Let's start a new life together without any baggage."

"Couldn't agree more, Mr Rohan Almeida."

With those words, both drove to Paul's apartment.

AN INDIAN TEENAGER'S DIARY

On an early morning in Poovar, a small town in Kerala, chaos continued in Meena Varma's house. Her *amma*, Rama, was unwell. Therefore Meena had woken up at 6 am to cook breakfast and lunch tiffin for herself, her *aniyan* and her *achan*.

She brought *stew* and *appam* to her *amma's* bed. "*Amma*, please eat something, I'll take you to the doctor after school."

"*Nanni*, Meena." Her *amma* thanked her.

"You do this for us every day. Today is my turn. I've made *sambar* and rice for lunch. Please eat on time. Bye."

Meena was a fourteen-year-old girl who was born and brought up in Poovar. She lived with her parents and her younger brother, Maarish. Her father Hari was a hardworking man and toiled in the paddy fields all day. He went to the nearby cities to sell his rice. They also owned a small general store that sold chocolates, groceries, biscuits, and other essential items. Her mother Rama looked after the shop, while Meena and Maarish also helped her. Meena was an obedient daughter and a sincere student in class. She had almond-shaped eyes and dark eyelashes, a broad nose, and big round lips. She had thick, long hair that was oiled tightly into two big plaits. She wore a dot of black *bindi* and applied a thin line of kajal under her eyes. Maarish, was eight and had a round chubby face. He respected his *chechi* and looked up to her as a role model.

Meena rushed to school, taking Maarish with her. She could not concentrate in class as "someone important" was missing in class today. Disappointed, she went back home for lunch.

Her *amma's* fever had increased. Meena took her to the doctor nearby. There were a lot of patients at the tiny clinic, so Meena guided her *amma* into a chair, and stepped outside.

And there he was, her "someone important," at the medical store opposite the clinic. Meena blushed. She would recognise him anywhere. Dressed in a red T-shirt and black pants, he looked cute. He was tall and had a lean body. He had an oval-shaped face with a tiny teenage moustache growing, and walnut-coloured skin. His smile, a bit crooked on the right was what stole Meena's heart. Just before he could turn and look at her, she heard her *amma's* name being called out.

"Rama Varma."

She went in. Putting an arm around her *amma*, Meena helped her to the doctor's cabin. The doctor prescribed medicine. As Meena and her *amma* were walking to the medical store, Meena looked around frantically.

"Looking for someone?" her *amma* asked her.

"No, no!" Meena replied, embarrassed.

They walked home quietly. The next day, Rama was ill again. Meena's *achan,* asked her to stay home and look after her *amma*, but Meena threw a tantrum, and her parents couldn't understand why.

Before things could get out of hand, Rama announced, "I'm better with the medicine, I'll manage for a couple of hours."

Hari didn't know why Meena was so upset over missing school because she'd skipped so many times in the past for frivolous reasons. Probably she'd changed and was committed to her studies, he thought.

But Rama knew the real reason. She smiled to herself. She was aware of her daughter's infatuation with Ajay. He was the son of their landlord, Mr Nair. He was quite a well-mannered and good chap. She knew that Meena's crush wouldn't last too long. Once she grew up, she'd have an arranged marriage to a boy that they would pick for her, someone who belonged to their caste. As long as she didn't break those rules, Rama didn't mind her having a crush on somebody for a few years. She knew that her daughter didn't have the courage to talk to a boy outside her family.

After reaching school, Meena eagerly waited for Ajay to enter the class. And there he was, just in time for class to begin. She could feel her heartbeat when she saw him.

Her friend, Madhu, asked for a pencil. She noticed that Meena's palms were moist. "Look at you all sweaty, Meena." She laughed.

Meena's face turned red.

"Sorry, I didn't mean to make you uncomfortable."

"I'm not uncomfortable, you're imagining stuff."

"Still in denial, poor girl!" said Madhu, as the class began.

After the classes were over and they began to walk home, Meena admitted to her infatuation. "I'm a bad girl."

"Why? It's not a crime to like a boy."

"No, it's not; but my *amma* is ill, and I left her to come to school."

"Just to catch a few glimpses of Ajay? That boy is really lucky, *huh?* Sacrifices have already been made for him."

"You're not making me feel any better. I'm feeling worse now."

"I'm just kidding, Meena. Go home. Your *amma* will be waiting for you."

When Meena reached home, her *amma* was in the kitchen, cooking. Meena threw her school bag aside and started to help out.

"I'm okay, Meena, don't worry." Her *amma* laughed.

"I'm so sorry for not staying at home today, *Amma*. I had an important topic in class that I couldn't miss."

"That's okay. I know how important school is to you. Freshen up. I'll serve you lunch."

The next few days were very exciting for Meena. They were going to go to Kovalam beach for the school picnic. She woke up early that morning, much before the alarm. She stuffed her bags with chips and chocolates, along with the lunch her *amma* had packed. Spending the whole day with Ajay was beyond exciting for her.

She took a shower and dressed in the uniform she had carefully ironed. She brushed her hair and powdered her face. Smiling in the mirror, she dreamt of various scenarios that could happen during the trip.

She is slipping into the water; Ajay saves her by grabbing her hand.

Or, the wind is blowing wildly, causing her scarf to fly away; Ajay rescues it and brings it back to her.

She blushed as she packed her scarf. She was watching too many Bollywood movies now.

She was caught smiling by Maarish, who went running to their *amma*.

Rama was in the dining room, serving breakfast.

"*Amma*, look at *chechi*. She's smiling to herself while packing her bag."

"*Chechi* loves picnics, just like you do," Hari replied.

"Yes, but I don't smile. Look, her face is red."

"Shut up, Maarish," said Meena, annoyed.

"Stop it, both of you," Rama said. "Eat your breakfast and go to school. Maarish, you'll also get your picnic next week."

The buses were lined up in front of their school, with number labels on them. Meena waited to see which bus Ajay got into, then dragged her friends to the same bus.

Thankfully, everyone was oblivious to the situation except for Madhu, who nudged her when they were sitting in the bus. "Look! Ajay is sitting in the front," she exclaimed.

"Oh, I hadn't noticed him," said Meena, trying to ignore her.

"So, was it a coincidence that you dragged us to this bus?" Madhu teased.

"Yes, of course."

"Let's go to the other one," Madhu said, pointing to the bigger bus next to them. "The seats are better there."

"I'm not moving from here," Meena retorted.

Madhu giggled.

As the bus began to move, everyone in the back cheered.

Ajay, who had turned backward, glanced at Meena who was looking at him adoringly, the wind blowing in her face. She looked down awkwardly when he looked at her and began to fidget with her fingers.

Madhu nudged her. "Ajay was just looking at you."

"You're imagining things."

"I know you were staring at him."

"Was it obvious?" Meena was red with embarrassment.

"So, you admit it?"

"I just looked at him once, and he saw me at the same time."

They stopped at the beach, and everyone played in the water. Meena managed to catch plenty of glimpses of Ajay. They all had lunch from their tiffin boxes and then returned home in the evening.

Meena had a lot of events to narrate back home at night. She followed her *amma* around the house, narrating the day in detail.

Final exams were approaching now. Meena was busy studying. She was one of the rank holders in her class. She caught glimpses of Ajay while writing her papers but made sure she wasn't distracted by him; she could not afford to lose a single mark.

Exams were over. It was vacation time. Rama usually visited her parents, who lived in the neighbouring town, but Meena wasn't in the mood to go. She wanted to be around Ajay. She couldn't imagine spending two months without seeing him. When Rama told Meena that she had to visit her grandparents', Meena threw a fit. She gave them the excuse of preparing for her board exams for next year. Her parents were shocked because she always loved visiting her grandparents. Finally, her *achan* agreed to pick her up after a couple of weeks. Madhu comforted her, saying that the two weeks would be over before she knew it. With a lot of tears, she left for her grandparents' place.

On the bus to her grandparent's town, Meena recollected the conversation she'd had with Madhu.

"So, you finally admit you're in love?"

"I don't know, but the thought of not seeing him for months makes me sad."

"You don't even attempt to talk to him and tell him how you feel."

"I cannot. I'm too scared; he might not feel the same way. Besides, our parents will never agree. You know we belong to different castes."

"So, this is how your love story is going to end. Nothing is going to ever happen?"

"Maybe God will help me out."

"*Haha.* You're funny, Meena."

"I just want to know if he likes me back. That's all I want for now. I'm happy just seeing him secretly for now."

The bus picked up speed. As the wind blew on Meena's face, she was reminded of the picnic. What a wonderful day that was!

She spent the rest of her vacation brooding. She wasn't her usual cheerful self which, she knew, worried her *amma*. But she knew that she would never confess what she felt. When the vacations were about to end, her mood was suddenly light. She was very happy to be back home.

She woke up early on her first day of school. But Ajay was nowhere in sight. Again, Meena's mood was down. Ajay finally made an appearance in class after a week. Meena was very excited that day. Her *amma* was starting to get worried about Meena's obsession with Ajay. She was concerned about the way she was affected by him.

Meena had spent over five years obsessing about Ajay now. She felt like this was true love. She had dreams about eloping with him because her parents would never agree to an inter-caste marriage. But she neither knew if he even liked her, nor did she attempt to find out. Was this how she wanted to end her love story?

Her friends noticed her moodiness and her anxiety. She would be chirpy the day she saw him. During vacations, she was withdrawn.

One day, Madhu came running to Meena with some news. "I'm afraid you're not going to like this."

"What?"

"Ajay and his family are moving to Chennai!"

"No!" cried Meena. She could feel the blood drain from her face.

"Meena, why don't you go and talk to him and tell him how you feel."

"No, I cannot. What if he rejects me? I won't be able to take it. Besides, he's moving now. It's all over." She threw her hands up.

Meena didn't take Ajay's move well. She cried at night and was sick the day he was moving. She was in bed all day and missed the last glimpse of him. She couldn't even say goodbye to him because they had never spoken to each other. She prayed to God that somehow, she would get him back. But as the days passed, her dreams of getting married to him began to fade. She began to lose interest in everything. One day she announced to her *amma* that she had no intention of getting married, ever. This came as a shock to her *amma*, but she did not say anything.

After their twelfth, Madhu had moved out of Poovar for her graduation to Trivandrum, and was staying in a hostel. They were going to start their final year in college. It was vacation time and Madhu had come home like she did every year. The girls had made their plans for the entire vacation.

During their second-last day of vacation, they sat in the paddy fields and ate their lunch. They had just finished a short trek to the temple at the base of the mountain.

Madhu said, "Ajay wanted me to give you this." She handed over an envelope.

"Who, Ajay? Ajay, as in our classmate Ajay?" Meena asked, fidgeting with her *dupatta*.

"Yes, Ajay, as in 'the love of your life,'" exclaimed Madhu.

"*Haha*! What has he given me?" Meena asked, opening the envelope.

"I'm sorry I hesitated to give you this. I was worried about things going wrong. I remember how you were depressed and didn't want to send you on that path again."

"Calm down, Madhu. I'm fine now."

"What is it? A letter?" asked Madhu.

"Yes. He says that he misses me and feels like there was a connection between us. I'll read it later."

"God! Meena. Isn't this a dream? I can't believe this love story. You've been dreaming of this day ever since school. It has finally come true! Do you know what that means?"

"What?"

"You know what! Why aren't you excited?"

"It's just a little weird since it's been so many years. By the way, he has even added his phone number below."

"I'm just excited to be a part of this love story. It can be made into a movie."

"Stop imagining things," said Meena as she got up and brushed dust off her dress.

"Where are you off to? You don't have to call him immediately." Madhu laughed.

"I just need some time. I want to read the letter alone."

"Sure. Meet me tomorrow at 8 am. I'm off after that."

"I will. Bye."

Meena went home and thought for a long time after she'd read the letter. She kept the letter in her bedside drawer. The next day she went to meet Madhu to say goodbye.

"So, did you call him? How did it go?" Madhu rubbed her palms together in excitement.

"No, I haven't." Meena smiled.

"Don't waste time. Hurry up."

"By the way, where did you meet Ajay?"

"I didn't. A friend of mine from college handed me the letter. That guy happens to be Ajay's friend, as well. Apparently, Ajay is studying at IIT Madras."

"Wow."

"Yeah. Nerdy boy, *huh?*"

Two months later, Meena graduated. Her parents were very happy. They invited the entire family over for dinner that night.

"Now that Meena has graduated, we should find a suitable groom for her," said her paternal grandfather during dinner.

"Yes. The coconut curry, rice, and *payasam* are all made by her. She is ready to settle down," Hari announced proudly.

"I know a family who stays in our town in Kovalam. Very good family. They will keep Meena happy," said Meena's maternal uncle.

"Please send me the boy's profile. I will get the horoscopes matched," said Rama excitedly.

"Wow, *Chechi*. You're going to be married soon. I will have our room to myself now," said Maarish.

"Shut up, Maarish," whispered Meena, kicking him under the table.

The horoscopes were checked the next day.

"Meena, your horoscopes have matched. Check his profile and photo," her *amma* said as she handed his profile and photo to her daughter.

"His name is Venkatraman. They own a big farm and a dairy. They distribute their products in and around the neighbouring town. They're very rich people."

"*Hmm*, I see," said Meena, inspecting the profile.

"Aren't you happy? You're going to be so close to us. It's going to be wonderful. Oh! I need to start the wedding preparations! Need to buy sarees; we need to buy jewellery as well. God knows what the price of gold is today."

"*Amma*, stop it."

"What? I'm getting prepared in my mind. Aren't you happy? Why don't you seem happy? Is something wrong?"

"*Amma*, nothing is decided yet. It's all so sudden."

"Okay, I will give you time. Meanwhile, let me call Venkat's *amma* and give them the good news."

A couple of days had passed. The boy's family was coming to see Meena the following day. Rama was busy cleaning the house and preparing a variety of dishes. Everything was going very well, but she was a little worried about Meena. She seemed very quiet. Was she unhappy? Was there anyone else in her mind? Was it Ajay? She was obsessed with him in school, but it had been years now.

Meena was taking a shower so Rama tiptoed into her room and began to look in her cupboard if there was something she could find. She went through all her contacts on the phone. She didn't find anything. As a last resort, she opened Meena's bedside drawers.

There was an envelope addressed to Meena. Shocked, she opened the letter.

Hi Meena,

I know it has been over five years since I moved away. I think we have some kind of a connection. I see you in every girl; I miss you every time I go to class. Even though we never spoke, your presence around me was overpowering. When I hear the word 'Poovar,' all I can think of is you and all the good memories of school. I hope you feel the same way about me...

Midway through the letter, Rama heard the bathroom room open. Hurriedly, she wrapped her *pallu* around the envelope.

"What are you doing here, *Amma*?"

"Nothing. Meena, please sit down. We need to talk."

"Anything serious?"

"Are you happy about getting married?"

"Yes, of course. I would have said something, otherwise."

"What is this, then?" she pulled out the envelope with tears in her eyes.

"Ajay wrote this letter for me. Madhu gave it to me. Don't be mad, *Amma*. Please."

"You don't feel the same way?"

"No *Amma*. Please don't cry."

"Are you sure? You don't need to hide anything from me. I know we are conservative and so don't prefer love marriages, especially from outside the caste. But I can fix it for you; I can talk to your *achan*. He won't agree immediately, but I will try. I knew how much you liked him in school and how upset you got when he moved away. For me, all that matters is my daughter's happiness."

"That won't be necessary, *Amma*. I have made my decision. I'm going to marry Venkat."

"What about Ajay? You refused to talk to anybody for months after he moved. I thought you might have forgotten about him, but you haven't. Besides, he likes you too."

"*Amma*, you are imagining things."

"I know my daughter."

"Okay, then let me make it very clear. I did like him in school. But I was a teenager, and it was just a crush. Now I'm over it."

"You are saying that because you're scared of us, Meena?"

"How can I love someone I have not even spoken to? I was stupid and silly. Besides, I don't want to move to a big city. He's obviously going to get a big job after his engineering and settle in Chennai."

"So what?"

"I want to continue living in a small town. I want the same life I've had since childhood. I don't want to go far away."

"But you don't know Venkat exactly, either."

"Yeah, but my family has picked him for me. I know you'll have made the perfect choice for me. Besides, we secretly had a couple of conversations over the phone. Maarish and *Ammavan* arranged it for me." Meena giggled.

"Then why are you so glum?"

"I'm going to be leaving you all, *Amma*. I'm going to miss you."

"*Aww*," said Rama as she hugged her daughter.

Everything was just her imagination after all she thought relieved. Teenagers don't understand love; it's just a small phase they go through. Everything was going to go fine. Her daughter was matured after all. She was going to be married to the guy of their choice which is every parents' dream she smiled to herself.

THE UNINVITED MOTHER

Viaan and Inaaya sat gloomily in the car as their dad, Hritesh, dropped them at school; it was their first day after the summer vacation.

"Excited about your first day kids?" Hritesh asked enthusiastically.

"It's the same old, Dad. Just a new class and a new teacher," replied Viaan.

"Yeah, and we are going to be in different classes this year." Inaaya frowned.

"I see. They shuffle everyone so that you make new friends." Hritesh smiled at them.

"I guess," replied both in chorus.

As they reached their school. Hritesh parked his car and walked them to the school gate. "Here," he said, handing their tiffin-boxes for lunch.

"Thanks, Dad."

"Mom's made some yummy cheese sandwiches, I hear."

"First of all, Dad, she's not our mom," snapped Viaan.

"Secondly, we don't like anything she makes," said Inaaya with a straight face.

Hritesh stood speechless as both of them walked away.

Back at home, Aarti waited anxiously for the kids to return home. As she looked out the window, her thoughts drifted back to her college days. The first time she'd seen Hritesh in her class. How handsome he looked, with his deep grey eyes, warm ivory coloured skin. How his silky-smooth hair fell on his forehead as he brushed it behind with his fingers. The crush she had on him! His amazing body, with strong-looking shoulders and broad chest. How she'd never had the courage to express her feelings for him. She remembered the sinking feeling she got when she learned that Hritesh was going abroad to pursue further studies. Then came the news that he got married to an American girl. She had then seen a Facebook post from him a year later announcing the birth of their twins. How happy they had both seemed. Aarti had felt a tinge of envy. Finally, trying to get on with her life, she got married. It was an arranged marriage.

A couple of months into marriage, her husband got himself into a financial mess, which led to his drinking. After that, he started to physically abuse her. She was with him for three years before she managed to get the courage to file for divorce and return to her parents' place.

One fine day, she ran into Hritesh at the supermarket in their colony. He told her that his kids were eight now and that his wife had recently passed away so he'd moved back to India and was living with his parents.

Aarti felt sorry for him. After that, she started visiting him and the kids regularly. Both were extremely cute and had their mom's blonde hair and dad's grey eyes. They had porcelain skin tone and pink cheeks. They had begun to grow very fond of her. She and

Hritesh had also become very good friends. Finally, she decided to propose to him.

"I want us to get married," she announced out of the blue, which came as a shock to Hritesh.

"But I have two kids, Aarti. I'm not sure if it's the right decision for them."

"I will raise them as my own. They need a mother, Hritesh," she said.

They got married after that. It was a small ceremony.

Hritesh and Aarti assumed that the kids would be happy after their wedding, but they weren't.

After they announced the wedding to the kids, everything changed. The kids were ten by then. They loved Aarti aunty but couldn't accept her as a mother. They said they were very happy, but their behaviour proved otherwise. Hritesh and Aarti took the kids on their honeymoon, where they refused to allow Aarti onto their bed.

When they returned home and Hritesh moved into a room with her, they broke several pieces of crockery. That was just the beginning of the tantrums, Aarti thought tearfully when she heard the doorbell ring. She ran to open the door, wiping away her tears.

"Hi Kids! How was your first day?"

"Umm, okay, I guess."

"Freshen up. I'll get you some chocolate milkshake and cheese dosas."

"Okay."

Back in their room, Viaan and Inaaya began to discuss Aarti.

"She seems a little low today," said Viaan.

"Yeah. Do you think dad told her about our comments on her cooking?" asked Inaaya.

"Probably, but who cares? She's not our mom. Serves her right for trying to pretend."

"Yeah."

Aarti waited for them at the dining table with their snacks. She smiled at them as they sat down.

They finished their meal quietly.

"So, shall I start looking at the syllabus for the year, and then we can get started on covering the books?"

"No thanks," snapped Viaan.

"I mean, dad will help us out once he's back. You can carry on with your evening walk," added Inaaya.

"But I don't mind doing it."

"It's our tradition. Dad always helps us with it."

"Okay, if you say so," said Aarti, trying to hide her disappointment.

During her evening walk, she discussed the incident with her friend Mona.

"Still no change, Mona. They refuse to let me in."

"You knew this wasn't going to be easy! It is going to take them time to accept you."

"It's almost a year now."

"It might take years. Be prepared for it."

"They hate me making their bed, they hate my cooking, and they hate everything I do. In short, they hate me."

"You're a great cook, and speaking of cooking, Myra would love for you to bake her a "Frozen" themed cake for her birthday."

"Really?"

"Yes." Mona smiled.

A couple of days later, at Myra's party, Viaan and Inaaya didn't seem to be enjoying anything. They sat in a corner and refused to partake in any of the activities and games organised. Aarti noticed that they hadn't touched the cake at all.

At night she finally narrated the incident to Hritesh as they lay in bed.

"They refused to even touch the cake I baked," she said with tears in her eyes.

"I'm sorry about it, Aarti, but if I try to talk to them it's only going to make things worse. Also, I want them to accept you wholeheartedly and not due to my pressure."

"I understand. I knew it was going to be difficult. Don't know why I'm getting so upset."

"You're doing your best. I don't know how long it is going to take for them to accept you, or if they will even accept you at all. This is not what we predicted; in the meanwhile, I think we should have a baby together. You deserve to be a mother," said Hritesh, smiling.

"We discussed this before we got married, Hritesh. Viaan and Inaaya are my kids too. I don't want any more. I don't want them to feel like they are being treated differently once we have a baby together."

"You should also think about yourself sometimes."

"Thanks, Hritesh, but my answer is still 'no.'"

"As you say, Madam." He smiled as he wrapped his arms around her.

The next evening when Aarti was cooking dinner, she overheard Viaan and Inaaya talking to their dad about a Parents' Day event at school.

"Dad, we would love for you to come. It's next week," she heard Viaan say.

"Sure, we both will make it to the event," Hritesh replied.

Then there was a sudden pause.

"But it's for the parents, and…" Inaaya whispered something.

"Yeah, Inaaya, your parents will be there."

"But Aarti aunty might be a little busy. She has a cake delivery on that day. I don't think she will be able to make it," Viaan said.

In response, Hritesh called out her name. "Aarti, could you come outside for a sec?"

"Coming," said Aarti. Wiping her hands with a kitchen napkin, she went to the living room.

"What are you doing Friday, next week? The kids say you have a cake to deliver?" asked Hritesh.

"I do," she said, nodding.

"The kids have a Parents' Day event that evening."

"We can drop the cake off on our way, or they could arrange a pickup." Aarti smiled.

"Great! Problem solved." Hritesh smiled at the kids.

"Okay," said Viaan in a soft tone and frowned at Inaaya.

At first, Aarti was a bit reluctant about going to the event but then she brushed off her thoughts saying that they would finally begin to accept her if she participated more in their life. She dressed in her favourite blue silk-cotton *salwar* suit. She wore matching blue studs, along with her favourite diamond *mangalsutra*. She looked extremely gorgeous in Indian attire, with her delicate features and black wavy hair that curled at the bottom. It was the first time that she was going to their school. They were going as a family. As a child, she had dreamed of a husband and two kids, a boy, and a girl. She never felt a sense of completion in her previous marriage because her first husband ill-treated her. But with Hritesh, it was different. Also, this could be the first step towards the kids accepting her. She smiled to herself in the mirror.

At the school, the auditorium was buzzing with people. The teachers were greeting the parents at the entrance. "Hi, Viaan and Inaaya! Finally, we meet your mom." Their class teacher smiled greeting Aarti.

"Stepmom," corrected Viaan.

After the kids introduced their friends to Hritesh and Aarti, they went backstage.

Viaan and Inaaya went to the green room where their friends had gathered.

"Your mom is so pretty," said Amaira.

"She's not our mom," snapped Inaaya.

"The way you described her, she sounded like a witch. But she seems sweet," said Snohit.

"Enough about her. Let us get ready for our performance," snapped Viaan.

Their class performed Shakespeare's play, "The Comedy of Errors." They enacted it perfectly. Viaan and Inaaya were the main characters in the play. After the play ended, the audience burst into loud applause. Hritesh and Aarti stood up and clapped with pride.

Were their friends' right after all? She did seem to be genuinely happy for them, thought Inaaya. She discussed it with Viaan that night.

"Do you think Aarti aunty loves us? She seemed to be genuinely happy watching our play."

"It's all fake. She's just trying to impress everyone, especially dad."

"Yeah, probably."

Aarti was very happy to be introduced to the kids' teachers as their stepmom. Finally, she was getting acknowledged by them in some way. She kept smiling that night as she went to bed.

After a couple of weeks, it was picnic day at their school. They were to be taken to Imagica at Lonavala.

Since they lived in Malad, it was quite a drive to Lonavala. Aarti wasn't very keen about Inaaya going because the girl had motion sickness, which also was the reason she couldn't go on any carnival rides.

Inaaya was never sent to picnics outside Mumbai; this was her first time, so she wanted to go.

Aarti tried to reason with Inaaya, but she wouldn't listen. Resigned, she handed Inaaya some pills for her motion sickness, asking her to take it before she got on the bus.

"Don't listen to her. She's trying to show us that she cares," Viaan warned her.

"Yes, I know. How can I miss my picnic? She's stupid," murmured Inaaya.

"Throw the pills away," Viaan instructed her.

The picnic turned out to be a disaster for Inaaya. Viaan, being in a different section of their class, was able to enjoy rides at the beginning. But he was forced to leave and take care of Inaaya, who had vomited at least eight times that day.

They reached school in the evening. They saw Aarti waiting for them anxiously.

Inaaya ran up to her and hugged her tightly. It was the first time she had done so after their marriage.

"What happened, Inaaya?" Aarti asked, concerned.

"I should have listened to you," Inaaya said, wiping her tears.

"Are you sick? How many times did you throw up?"

"Eight. I can barely stand. I want to go home, Mom."

Aarti froze. Her daughter finally used the "M" word. It felt like music to her ears. She'd waited for more than a year to hear that.

"I'm so sorry the tablet didn't help," Aarti said, taking them both to the car.

"What happened?" asked Hritesh. He was waiting in the car in the driver's seat.

"I did not listen to mom and threw away the pills she'd given me. Ended up puking eight times. Serves me right," muttered Inaaya.

Hritesh smiled at Aarti. He noticed that his daughter had finally begun to accept their stepmother, unlike Viaan who seemed frustrated at Inaaya's sudden acceptance of Aarti.

"Don't worry, Inaaya. Mom will take care of you," he said.

That night Aarti fed Inaaya in her bed. Inaaya refused to leave Aarti, sleeping in their room, while Hritesh slept with Viaan in his room.

This was the first time in years that Inaaya had fallen sick. Hritesh's mother always made sure they never travelled long distances by road. They respected their grandma, but with Aarti it was different. Anyway, now half the job was done. It was only Viaan who had to accept Aarti, thought Hritesh.

"I asked her to throw the pills away," said Viaan, interrupting Hritesh's thoughts.

"Why was that?"

"Aarti aunty tries to act as our mom but she's not."

"But Viaan, you loved her before we got married, so we assumed you would be happy to have her as part of the family."

"We're happy for you, but we don't need a mom."

"Does that mean I made a mistake by marrying her? I did it for you. You both were very young when you lost your mom and you both seemed to like Aarti so much."

"Yes, we did, but we didn't know she had an ulterior motive. We don't need a stepmom, Dad. I don't know why Inaaya has suddenly changed sides. She will come to her senses soon."

"There are no sides, Viaan. Is this how you're going to behave with her all your life? She's been nothing but kind to you. She loves you both."

"Please don't support her, Dad. It's all fake. She did all the drama of being nice because she wanted to marry you. She is not our real mother! She can never be."

She can never be.

The words haunted Hritesh. He was glad that Inaaya had started to accept Aarti, but he was afraid Viaan wouldn't crack so easily.

Things began to get difficult from then on. Viaan tried to draw a wedge between Aarti and Inaaya, which made Inaaya falter a lot. Sometimes she'd make plans to go shopping with Aarti, or allow Aarti to drive her to haircuts and dental appointments, but many times she would make an excuse not to go. Aarti showed neither hurt nor anger, but Hritesh was starting to get impatient.

"Viaan is trying to manipulate Inaaya," he told Aarti.

"They're kids, Hritesh. What do you expect from someone who's only twelve?" Aarti retorted.

"It's been almost two years since we got married, and you do so much for them. You deserve better."

"This isn't about me, Hritesh. I only married you for the children."

Hritesh stared at her.

"*Haha!* I mean I do love you now, you know," Aarti began to laugh.

"Then let's make a baby, Aarti. I want you to be happy. My kids are never going to accept you. I don't want you to lose your chance of being a mother. You're almost forty now."

"You make me sound so old. I'm thirty-eight, to be precise, and I am a mother. Trust me, they'll come around." She smiled.

Hritesh admired Aarti's patience. He recollected their first day as a family after they got married. The kids wouldn't allow their dad to be with Aarti. They slept in his bed for months.

At last, Hritesh had to ask them to move to their room. They had been angry with him and had called his parents over to come and stay with them, cutting Aarti off from the kitchen. Only his mother was allowed to feed them and take care of them. His mother felt sorry for Aarti but couldn't do anything against the kids' wishes. Finally, she had told them that she had to return home. After that, they refused to eat what Aarti made for them. Whenever Aarti dressed beautifully and Hritesh had complimented her, her jewellery disappeared or her dress was found damaged the next day. There were times when Aarti burned her hands by touching a hot iron kept on her bed or a hot pan left in the kitchen tray on purpose.

Aarti seemed to be undisturbed by anything the children put her through, but Hritesh felt guilty. Those incidents had started to happen again now. Hritesh couldn't believe how bad his children were behaving.

Initially, he'd given them a chance because they had lost their mom at a young age, but now it was too much for him to take.

"What is this?" shouted Hritesh one day when he found Aarti's diamond *mangalsutra* in their dustbin. As he went to take it out, he noticed that her jewellery and makeup kit were thrown away.

"I don't know," said Viaan with a straight face.

"How did this land here?"

"I don't know, Dad," he said curtly.

"You don't have the courage to even own up! Is this how I've raised you? This behaviour is immature and unacceptable. I will not tolerate such nonsense anymore."

"What happened?" asked Inaaya in shock as she entered their room.

"Do you know about this? Are you involved in this as well?"

"No, Dad. I didn't do it this time."

"You mean earlier you were involved in all this?"

Inaaya hung her head in shame.

Aarti followed Inaaya in. "What's going on?" she asked, puzzled.

"Viaan, could perhaps explain it to us?" said Hritesh.

"I cannot take this anymore, Dad," shouted Viaan.

"Cannot take what?" asked Hritesh.

"This pretence of showing everyone that we're a family. Here's the truth, Dad. We are not happy with Aarti aunty. You wanted to get married, you got married. But that doesn't mean we need to accept her as well. We are never going to. Stop pushing her on us. We don't like her; she pretends to be nice to us but she doesn't love us. She is not our mother. She can never be."

"Enough. I have given you too much freedom," said Hritesh. Furious, he raised a hand to slap Viaan.

Aarti caught his hand. "No, Hritesh. I think they have had enough. We cannot force them to accept me. It's been two years now. We tried and failed. We decided to get married because they needed a mother, and not because we needed each other. If they are unhappy, there's no point in us being together." She left the room in tears.

She quickly packed her bags and left without saying goodbye.

Hritesh went to his room and locked the door.

It was Inaaya who broke the silence.

"Viaan, I think this is enough. We need to stop the drama."

"She isn't our mother, Inaaya, please understand."

"By blood, no. But who is a mother, anyway? Somebody who puts our needs before her own. Somebody who sacrifices her sleep for us. She wakes up early each morning to pack tiffins that we don't bother to eat. She always wants to help us with our school projects and homework, but we don't allow her to. She makes our bed in the morning after we go to school, she cleans our room. She waits by the window every day for us to return from school, eagerly waiting to know about our day, which we shared before dad and she were married. She cares about us. She wants us happy. She is the one we look up to as a sense of security, someone who is teaching us the difference between right and wrong, someone who understood us right from the beginning. She has never judged us. If this isn't a mother, Viaan, who is? Now don't tell me she didn't give us birth and did everything to just marry dad. She is already married to him now, and he loves her. Why would she continue to pretend even now? She's been waiting patiently for us to accept her."

Meanwhile, Aarti sat gloomily at her parents' house.

"We've always wanted you to be happy, Aarti," her mother said, wiping her tears.

"I know *Aai*, but they are not happy with me. They haven't been able to accept me," Aarti said, trying to hold back her tears.

"My poor child! First the beating husband, and now these kids acting this way with you. *Tuzza nasheebachz kharaab aahe, Balaa.*" Her mother cried bitterly.

"*Aai*, please. I'm already upset. Don't be melodramatic."

"I'm sorry, dear. You did your best, I know. But it didn't work, probably it was never meant to be. What did Hritesh say about this?" her father asked her.

"Hritesh was about to slap Viaan when I told him I was leaving. He was too shocked to say anything."

"He's caught in between. I hope you understand that he will always support his kids. They will always be his priority. You knew this when you took the plunge. We thought that the kids adored you. You never told us any of this. They seemed okay when we were around."

"No, they weren't, but I always thought they'd come around. I thought Inaaya had accepted me, but she kept wavering. I did my best, *Baba*."

"I know you did. May I ask you a question?"

"Yes, *Baba*."

"You never thought of having your child?"

"*Baba*, you're seriously asking me this? Viaan and Inaaya are my children. Maybe they don't consider me their mom, but for me, they are my kids."

The doorbell rang. Aarti's father got up and opened the door. He was shocked to see Viaan and Inaaya.

"Hi Grandpa, is mom here?" asked Inaaya.

"Yes, of course. Come in."

"Hi, is it too late?" asked Viaan.

"It's never too late," Aarti said, hugged both of them tightly as tears rolled down her eyes.

"What does that mean?" asked Aarti's mother, confused.

"Mom taught us a lot of things when we were little and she used to come and visit us at Granny's place. One of them is, 'You should respect time, and the people who value you,'" said Inaaya.

"I used to always fight with my best friend, Reyaansh. When he left for Bangalore, I realised his worth. But it was too late then. Now, I didn't want to be late. Like last time," said Viaan quietly.

"When you got married to dad, we thought we'd lose him to you," Inaaya confessed. "We always thought you both would have your kids someday, and we would be the step-children. We thought you just pretended to love us so that you could marry dad. And he was so into you. The way he adores you, and you're so pretty. I was extremely jealous. I can never be as beautiful as you ever. I was blinded by envy."

"Baby, I married dad to be with you kids, and not the other way around. And speaking of more kids. I have two already. They are a handful!" Aarti smiled. "And you are beautiful, Inaaya. Wish you could see yourself through my eyes, Honey."

"On this lovely occasion let us have some chocolate muffins, your favourite. We bought them last night because we had plans to visit you kids today," said Aarti's mother, disappearing into the kitchen.

"How did you kids get here? Does dad know you are here?" asked Aarti, turning back to the kids.

"Dad drove us," said Inaaya.

"Where is he now?"

"Oh, he'll be here in some time." Inaaya smiled.

"Why?"

"Viaan told him to get your *mangalsutra* fixed after dropping us off. He went to Pethe jewellers."

An hour later, Hritesh was back with Aarti's *mangalsutra*.

"Here," he said as he handed it over to Aarti.

They both smiled at each other.

THE SPILLED CUP OF CAPPUCCINO!

When Ayaan Mehra woke up in the morning, he could literally feel gravity. He struggled to get out of bed, like any other day. The gravity, along with nausea and headache, was too much to take. The combination of last night's hangover.

With great effort, he brushed his teeth and walked into the dining room. "Extra cheese omelette *aur ek* strong coffee, *dena*," he instructed his cook, holding his head in his hands.

"*Bhaiya, ek aspirin de dun?*" she asked him.

"*Mein leta hu,*" he said. Reaching into a cabinet, he unscrewed the cap and popped a pill into his mouth.

"*Pehle naastha toh karlijiay,*" she said, handing him his breakfast.

She watched as he snatched the plate and stuffed the breakfast in his mouth. This was Ayaan's usual ritual. He was always hungover in the mornings. His face looked the colour of a ripe cherry tomato in the morning with the hangover. His thick black hair was messed up as it had overgrown. He badly needed a haircut and a shave. He looked much more decent when he'd moved in to Mumbai. He dressed in shorts and t-shirts that had begun to fit him tight on the tummy thanks to his growing potbelly.

She went to clean up, and found a huge bottle of whiskey in the living room and left-over plates of chicken legs, wondering if this lifestyle was ever going to end. She had seen a lot of bachelors in her life, but they all settled at some point in time. With Ayaan, this had been going on for more than five years now. There was no change in his lifestyle. Initially, when he had a job, this behaviour was only seen on weekends. But after he quit his job to do some work on his laptop back home, this happened almost every day.

That evening, Ayaan went to his usual place, Café Coffee Day. He ordered his regular cappuccino and began to work on his laptop. He was expecting Harpreet, his friend, and ex-colleague from his previous company.

"Hi Ayaan."

"Hi Harpreet," said Ayaan.

"How are you doing, man?" Harpreet said, shaking his hand vigorously and pulling him into a hug.

"I'm good, man. How are you?"

"Sabh changa hai, ji."

"So, how's work going? Does anybody miss me?" asked Ayaan.

"Hahaha. You must be joking, dude. It's almost been a year since you quit. People don't need even a couple of weeks to replace someone."

"Yeah, true that."

"So, how is your screenplay writing coming?"

"Very well. But no breakthrough though."

"These things take time. Do you want me to talk to Jeetu and help you get back the job just until…?"

"No, no. I hate that place. You know how they treated me. I felt like shit. They don't deserve me."

"Dude, your smoke breaks were increasing, and you were taking too many holidays. Maybe if you could…"

"Enough with the lecturing. Nobody understands me. People with talent always struggle."

"I understand, but you need to pay rent, and your expenses are so much. I'm just saying you need some job till you find something you like. I'm not telling you to come back, but there are a million other jobs. Look, I'm worried about you. That's all. You told me about your money problems, that's why I'm saying this. You said you were awkward about borrowing money from your parents every month."

"Enough. You're talking to me like I am a loser whose parents take care of his expenses. This is what happens in our country. No place for talent."

"Dude, I didn't mean that. I was just…"

"I thought at least someone understood me, man. But I was wrong. Please leave, dude. Please, right now."

Without saying a word further, Harpreet walked out, leaving everyone staring.

Ayaan felt even more frustrated now. Although the things Harpreet had said weren't wrong, he didn't need to be more demoralised than he already was.

Just then he noticed a pretty girl enter the café. She had a wheatish complexion and dark brown hair that was pulled back into a ponytail. She had thick, long eyelashes with soft eyes and a dainty nose. She was dressed in a plain black t-shirt and blue jeans. She had the most casual look and yet managed to look beautiful even without makeup. So rare to see a girl like that these days, thought Ayaan to himself.

As he was watching, she ran into another customer, spilling his cup of hot coffee on his shirt. He was an old man of about sixty, with a wrinkled neck and a honey-coloured face. He had grey hair and a handlebar moustache. He was dressed in a neat-ironed ivory shirt and grey trousers.

"You stupid kids these days, so engrossed in your smartphone," he barked at her in a voice loud enough for everyone to hear.

"So sorry, Uncle. Please let me buy you another coffee," she said and hurried to the counter grabbing some tissues.

"I'm already late," he shouted.

'What a grumpy old fellow!' thought Ayaan. He got up and offered the man a seat at his table while the girl went to order another coffee for him.

"What am I going to do by waiting? I am already late," he shouted at Ayaan.

Ayaan looked at the girl, who helplessly tried to hurry the staff to make the coffee quickly.

"Forget it. I will tell my daughter I'm not coming," the man said and sank into the chair.

"I'm sorry, Uncle," said the girl.

"I'm Ritu, by the way," she said, introducing herself to Ayaan and the man. She dragged a chair to their table.

"Hi, I'm Ayaan." Ayaan held out his hand and vigorously shook Ritu's.

"Let go of the girl, Ayaan. You guys pounce on any pretty girl you see," said the old uncle, sounding annoyed.

All of them burst into laughter.

"You think I'm pretty, Uncle? Thank you," said Ritu, beaming.

"I need to thank you for saving me from the awful party today," confessed the man, shaking his head.

"Why is that, Uncle?" asked Ayaan curiously.

"Long story. By the way, I am Ashok."

The waitress appeared with two cappuccinos.

"Cool, now we can hear your story as we sip coffee," said Ritu.

"My wife and I are separated," began Ashok. "My daughter insists we all meet for her son's birthday every year."

"I don't understand what's wrong with that," asked Ritu, puzzled.

"It's too much melodrama. Why can't we meet our daughter separately? Mohini, my wife, loves to create a scene in front of everyone and then starts crying. Women can cry so much. Gosh! No offence to you, Ritu."

"None taken."

"Then why were you so frustrated, Uncle? You said you were getting late, right?" asked Ayaan.

"That's because I was late to the airport and Mohini would accuse me of missing it on purpose and create more drama. But when I sat down, I realised that she is not my wife anymore, and I'm done trying to please her. That is why I thanked Ritu."

"That's quite a story, Uncle," said Ritu. "The reason I was so distracted today, well, I just broke up with my boyfriend. He was too controlling. My parents set him up for me."

"We're listening," said Ayaan with full attention.

"I come from a family of achievers. My parents are both doctors. My brother and sister both are pursuing medicine as well. And I just finished my B.A. with great effort."

"Wow. What a family. What fields are they in?" asked Ashok, curious.

"Well, dad is a cardiologist, mom is a paediatrician. Can someone ask about me, sometimes?" said Ritu, sarcastically.

"Sorry, Ritu. Please go on," said Ashok.

"So, they set me up with a family friend. He's currently pursuing his M.D."

"So, what's the problem here?" asked Ayaan impatiently.

"There's no chemistry between us. It's like a business setup. We both don't love each other. Besides, he's a replica of my dad. So controlling! I couldn't take it anymore. So, I ran away from home before they could discover my breakup!"

"I'm sure that's not a solution for this, Ritu," said Ashok gently.

"I have already made up my mind."

"How are you going to manage? Where would you stay? Do you have a job?" asked Ayaan.

"I have spoken to a friend. She stays alone. I'll be moving in with her. And I will find a job soon. Anyway, tell us about you now, Ayaan."

"There's nothing to share. I'm just a big loser trying to get a break in my career."

"*Uh-uh*. That explains the lazy stubble," laughed Ritu.

"I quit my job wanting to make it big. But now I'm just a loser whose parents pay his rent."

The three chatted for half an hour more and then parted ways, promising to be in touch after Ritu created a WhatsApp group. Little did they know that the cup of cappuccino would change each of their lives.

They met again after a month at the same CCD. Ritu had found a job after a month of rigorous search. She was hired as an editor in a magazine. The three of them had become very close by then, chatting regularly in the group. Ashok sent them various videos, Ritu was always giving them celebrity gossip, and Ayaan was the one with all news updates. There wasn't a time they did not talk about their day, and how Mumbai was getting more crowded by the day.

That evening Ayaan seemed very low.

"I'm happy you have a job now, but I feel so useless. My writing is going nowhere and I'm living off my parents' money. Should I get back to corporates?"

"Ayaan, this is just a bad phase. You don't need to do stuff you do not like. I am sure you will figure out something soon."

"Guess who called me up today?" asked Ashok, all of a sudden changing the topic.

"Who?" asked both.

"Mohini."

"Why?"

"I don't know. She just spoke to me casually. She also mentioned that she missed me at a barbeque party last night."

"You are fond of barbeques?" asked Ayaan.

"Yeah, I'm sort of an expert at barbeques."

"Do you think she's lonely and misses you?" asked Ritu.

"It's too late now, Ritu. Besides, I'm very happy now."

"Realisation has started to dawn on her. It won't be too long before you realise the same, Uncle," said Ayaan. "Life is too short to spend it alone."

"Yes, Uncle. Now you are capable enough to take care of yourself. Once you get older, things will get tougher," Ritu added.

"You kids don't know anything about marriage. I have a life. I need peace."

"Okay, okay, let us change the topic now," Ritu said. "Shall we catch a movie at say six? I've heard 'Bala' is really funny. Should be a nice change for us. What do you guys think?"

"Yeah, I don't mind," said Ayaan.

"I'm in, too. I love Ayushmaan's movies," said Ashok, and the three left after Ashok insisted on paying the bill.

Ritu had begun to enjoy life since her job. She was very happy with her career and personal life. She could eat take-outs and hang out with her friends without any restrictions. She'd never had pyjama parties in her life before. This was the best time in her life. She was happy with her newfound freedom. She no longer had to force herself to hang out with the guy her parents had fixed for her, or attend the family gatherings she so hated.

Ayaan's life continued to be the same, except for the guilt that had been piling up each day. His social circle was almost zero now. He'd stopped going on social media. He refused to talk to his parents as he was too ashamed and embarrassed, even though they were comfortable paying his rent and taking care of his expenses. The only people he chatted with were Ashok and Ritu.

As for Ashok, he was a happily single man. He watched cricket all day and had beer with his friends in the evenings.

During their next meet, Ashok and Ritu were quite happy and chirpy. They joked and laughed a lot. Ayaan was quiet, which kept bringing the group's mood down.

"What's the matter, Ayaan?" Ritu finally asked.

"It's just that the guilt is killing me," Ayaan finally admitted.

"You are not answerable to anyone; your parents don't mind and you know that," said Ashok.

"Yeah, good that your family is loaded," added Ritu.

"But I don't feel good," admitted Ayaan.

"Well, in that case, you must find a job. I know you'll hate to hear this but that's your only option," said Ritu.

"I thought at least you guys had faith in me," said Ayaan disappointed.

"To be honest, Ayaan, we don't know anything about your work," said Ashok.

"Well, in that case, let me share my script with you guys."

"Yeah, that would be good. Anyway, I've got to get going now. I need to shop. I've got a date tonight." Ritu blushed as she got up from her seat.

Ayaan waited patiently for a week for the feedback from his friends.

Finally, after a week, came Ritu's reply. "I've read it, shall we catch up this Sunday and talk?"

"Did you like it?" asked Ayaan.

"We'll talk," replied Ritu.

Ayaan had begun to worry now. He sensed something was off. He waited anxiously at their hangout. To kill time, he ordered his regular cappuccino. Half an hour later, he finally saw Ritu.

"Hi, Ayaan." She smiled.

"So? What do you think?" he asked anxiously.

"Let us wait for Ashok uncle, Ayaan," she said signalling to the waitress for her coffee.

She seemed very distracted, texting someone, blushing, and constantly checking her hair and lipstick on her phone.

"What's going on with you? Why are you so distracted?" Ayaan was irritated.

"Oh, I'm meeting the same guy tonight. I think it's going somewhere." She blushed.

"Whatever," grumbled Ayaan.

"Why are you so frustrated?"

"You are making me wait so much, Ritu."

"Here comes Ashok uncle," said Ritu, rubbing her hands.

Once they had greeted Uncle, Ritu said, "So, I read your script, Ayaan. Let me tell you honestly, the script is quite gripping. The characters are amazing, too. But... here comes the part I hate to tell you." She took a deep breath. "The stories are nothing new. The ending is predictable. It's nothing that the audience hasn't seen before. What do you think, Ashok uncle?"

"You are right, Ritu. I felt like I've seen this stuff before. It's just recreated with new characters and modern scenarios."

"It's not that easy to write, you guys. Most of my friends say that they love my script and it's just a matter of luck."

"Are they your real friends, Ayaan? You need someone to give you honest feedback. The world is very competitive. You cannot be just good. You have to be the best," said Ashok.

"You guys aren't supportive at all. I hate that I'm alone, with nobody to support me." Ayaan got up angrily, threw a five-hundred rupee note, and stormed off.

Ritu and Ashok stared at each other.

"What was that about?" asked Ritu, her eyes wide.

"I don't know. Your generation, I tell you. Cannot hear the truth."

"Forget him. Let me tell you about Rohit."

"Who's Rohit?"

"My date, Uncle. You forgot?"

"Yes, yes. I do remember. Please tell me. I've got a lot of time to kill before the India-Pakistan match starts."

Ayaan spent the next month avoiding Ritu and Ashok. He even exited from their WhatsApp group. One day, he finally got a call from his agent to discuss his latest script. The old ones seemed to be going nowhere. He told Ayaan that his stories were no good. The agent said that he loved Ayaan's style of writing and the characters, but this script would never be selected and he needed to come up with new stuff.

This was the same feedback that Ritu and Ashok Uncle had given him.

This was it.

Ayaan couldn't take it anymore. Nausea began to hound him. He began to throw up more often. The sleepless nights got worse; he had managed to cut off from the world again. Ritu and Ashok uncle had made him feel better for a few months. Now it was there again, the depression. His reckless drinking started again, and the endless smoking. He began to eat less and drink more. The sleeping pills weren't even a little bit effective; insomnia began to creep in at night.

As for Ritu, her life had begun to feel alien now. She started to feel uncomfortable with her flatmate Sonia's lifestyle. Boys were constantly at her apartment. First, it was only her friends, but now it was her constant one-night stands. She was growing fed up with the half-naked dudes in their living room. Every weekend there was a party. Ritu drank occasionally but didn't like the idea of getting wasted or handling drunk, puking people. On top of it, she had a dirty apartment to clean on Sunday mornings. Her boyfriend, Rohit was becoming a problem too. She'd enjoyed the initial stage of dating, but now he was always showing up at her doorstep. He always wanted to hang out in her room. Ritu wasn't comfortable taking a guy to her bedroom. She always made excuses of being hungry, taking him out to restaurants. But how long could she keep doing that? He had hinted about getting physical, but she had never done this before. She just wanted to make sure she was in love; she wasn't a girl who was comfortable having casual relationships.

Finally came the day when Rohit lost his cool.

It was a Friday night, and Rohit dropped in at Ritu's place at 10 pm, as usual, unannounced. Ritu had just finished eating Maggi while watching "Friends" on Comedy Central, her stress buster.

"Surprise!" He smiled, holding up a blue box of cookies from Sweetish House Mafia.

"Thanks, I was just going to sleep."

"You don't seem happy to see me. I got your favourite double choco-chip cookies," Rohit said disappointed, sitting on her couch.

"I love the cookies, thank you. I'm just sleepy," said Ritu, opening the box and taking a bite of the cookie.

"Okay. Where is Sonia?" he said, looking around.

"Oh, she's gone to Goa with her friends."

"Wow, so we have the apartment to ourselves," said Rohit, planting a kiss on Ritu's cheek.

"What do you mean?"

"I mean, I could maybe stay over here this weekend?"

"Why?"

"Don't you like having me around, Ritu?"

"It's not like that. I'm not comfortable with all this."

"What do you mean by 'all this?'"

"I'm a very simple girl, Rohit. I don't sleep around with people."

"I'm not people, Ritu. I am your boyfriend. Is there someone else? Please tell me honestly."

"No, no. I am not comfortable getting things to a physical level yet, Rohit."

"It's almost been a month, Ritu. It's not the 19th century anymore. Don't tell me all this nonsense. I am sure there is someone else. Tell me who? Is it that Ayaan guy whom you keep talking about all the time?"

"No. He is just a friend," Ritu said angrily.

"Stop all this nonsense. I've had enough. If you didn't want to sleep with me, why did you lead me on? Wasted so much of my time. Don't give me this bullshit excuse now. Girls aren't the *purane-khayalat-ke-sati-saavitri* types anymore."

"That's not true, Rohit. You cannot accuse me of leading you on. I'm not that type of girl. Trust me. I think we should take things slow."

"Slow? My foot. We are done here. You are a cheating and lying whore," said Rohit, getting up. He slammed the door behind him.

Ritu stood in the hallway, crying. How had she landed herself in such a bad situation? She needed somebody to console her, to tell her that she was a nice girl. But the empty apartment stared at her. She knew where she had to go. She grabbed her wallet and keys and left.

Meanwhile, Ashok was leading a banal life. He was starting to get bored now. The endless cricket matches on TV. Having beers whenever he felt like it. At first, it had seemed freeing. He hung out with his friends whenever he wanted to. There was no one to taunt him or make him change his plans. But now it felt all the same. He ate sweets whenever he felt like it. He thought it would be fun, but now it didn't seem exciting as there was no thrill in doing that. He skipped showering every other day and stopped wearing clean clothes, but that wasn't fun either. Everything seemed monotonous. He began to miss Ritu and Ayaan too. They'd become so close over the months, and it had been weeks since they'd met. He wished they hadn't given Ayaan honest feedback. Suddenly his phone started ringing. It was Ritu.

"Hi, Ritu. I was just thinking of you. Hundred years, *Beta*," he said smiling.

"Uncle, please come to Ayaan's apartment," she said, sobbing.

"What happened? Is everything okay?"

"Ayaan isn't opening the door."

"He must be out of town."

"The neighbours haven't seen him step out for days. Milk packets and newspapers are lying outside the door."

"I'm coming right away."

Ashok reached Ayaan's house as soon as he could. Ayaan lived in Oshiwara which was close to Ashok's apartment in Lokhandwala. There were a few neighbours at the door. Ritu ran to him the minute he arrived. They had called a person to break the lock by then. They opened the door and ran inside. Ayaan was lying on his bed. They tried to wake him, but he wasn't getting up. Ritu immediately called an ambulance, and they rushed him to the nearest hospital.

Ritu and Ashok waited outside as the doctors examined him.

After a seemingly long wait, the doctor stepped outside. "Seems like an overdose of sleeping pills. We need to inform the police since it seems like an attempted suicide case. Are you his immediate family? We need you to sign some papers."

"No, he would never commit suicide. We know him very well. Let us just talk to him once, please," Ritu protested.

"Are you related to him?"

"Yes, I'm his sister, and this is our dad," lied Ritu.

Ashok gave her a hard stare.

"Why would you lie to the doctor?" he muttered to Ritu once they were allowed to go inside.

"*Shh*, we cannot let his family know."

Ayaan was lying on the bed with an IV attached to his hand. He had tears in his eyes when he saw the two of them. "How did you guys find me? I'm so sorry about everything. I feel like shit. My family cannot know about this," he cried.

"Calm down, Ayaan. We are your family now," Ritu winked, putting her hand on his.

"What?"

"Ritu told the doctors that we are your immediate family. They were about to call the police as it seemed like attempted suicide," Ashok explained.

"My family cannot know about this, please. I did not try to commit suicide. I passed out due to an overdose of sleeping pills. I cannot put my parents under any more stress. As it is, they worry about me."

"No worries Ayaan, we will take care of everything. You should be able to go home by evening."

"I'm not comfortable with this whole thing," Ashok said. "How can you hide something so major from your parents?"

"Major, yes, if he was trying to commit suicide, but it was just an accidental overdose, Uncle. Ayaan, promise us that you won't take those pills again."

"I promise."

"How can we believe him?"

"We can, by staying over with him. Let's make sure he gets better. Few months we don't talk and look what happens to the guy. My life hasn't been that great, either."

"Yeah, I'm really sorry. I cut you guys off. I miss you," Ayaan confessed.

"Okay. I could use a change, myself. Let's take care of each other," said Ashok.

After a lot of struggle, Ritu was able to convince the doctor not to file an FIR. Since Ayaan was completely fit, they let him go home the same day. It was nice for them all to stay together. Ritu stayed in Ayaan's room, while Ashok and Ayaan settled on the couch. Ritu was happy to get a break from the half-naked boys and the parties. She was very comfortable with Ayaan and Ashok uncle. Ayaan was happy to have his friends over. He didn't need to take sleeping pills anymore. As for Ashok, he was happy that he wasn't alone anymore. A month passed.

One day, Ritu finally said, "It's almost been a month now. I think I must return home."

"But where will you go? You hate the flat you stay in, currently. Besides, I'm having a great time. I don't want you guys to leave," said Ayaan.

"Ayaan, you're much better now. I think we have stayed long enough. It even looks inappropriate," said Ashok.

"C'mon, you guys. We are good friends. Who cares what anyone thinks?" said Ayaan.

"Yes, Ayaan. But it's not only about other people. We cannot stay here forever. And Ritu, I hate to say this again and again, but I think it's high time you returned home. Your parents must be upset. Nobody just leaves their house like that," Ashok said.

"Let me give it a thought."

"I also feel that you should talk to your parents, Ritu. You hated this kind of lifestyle," added Ayaan.

"But I hate everything about my family."

"You need to talk, Ritu. There is nothing better than having a heart-to-heart conversation and clearing things up. It's about adjusting and hearing out your family, and not breaking relationships up over petty issues," said Ashok.

"Really, Uncle? Are you really saying that? What about you? Didn't you just leave your wife because you thought she was 'nagging?'" said Ritu, using her fingers to make air quotes.

"That's completely different," protested Ashok.

"No, Uncle. Ritu is right. I feel like life is too small to waste it on little things," Ayaan added.

"As far as you're concerned," Ritu said, "you need to step out of your apartment, dude. You look like shit. Look at your overgrown beard."

"I'm not ready. People stare at me. It's like everyone judges me."

"Don't you think it's your judgement about yourself?" asked Ritu.

"Yes, Ayaan. You cannot wait forever; you need to start making a living. You have spent enough time trying to write. If things aren't materialising, doesn't mean you just give up. Continue to write, but you need to start doing a job, meanwhile. It's high time," said Ashok.

"Yeah. Hasn't it been like two years already?"

"One and a half," corrected Ayaan.

"Whatever."

After a couple of days, Ritu and Ashok moved out.

Ritu told her flatmate that she would be returning home. Her parents were overjoyed to have her back. She spoke to her parents and told them how she felt. They agreed that they had pushed her hard due to peer pressure, and said that Ritu was free to choose her career and a life partner whenever she met one and that they would always support her life choices.

Ashok finally called his wife and asked her to meet him for dinner. She was surprised by the way Ashok treated her. She'd always felt like he never heard her out, but this dinner was different. Ashok paid attention to all the tiny things she said. He finally told her how his life was empty without her, and that he could now understand that the "nagging" was just a part of her love for him. They decided not to go for the divorce after all.

For Ayaan, it took him a lot of months, but finally, he was able to get a decent job. Things hadn't materialised for his writing yet, but he was very happy that he was able to stand on his feet. He still waited for the "call" that would make his dreams come true.

Three strangers, who had now become best friends, were able to change each other's lives.

They all had one thing to thank: that spilled cup of cappuccino!